S·U·M·M·E·R L·I·G·H·T

OTHER BOOKS BY ROXANA ROBINSON

Georgia O'Keeffe: A Life

A Glimpse of Scarlet and Other Stories

HARDSCRABBLE BOOKS—FICTION OF NEW ENGLAND

Laurie Alberts, *The Price of Land in Shelby*

Thomas Bailey Aldrich, *The Story of a Bad Boy*

Chris Bohjalian, *Water Witches*

Dorothy Canfield Fisher (Mark J. Madigan, ed.),
Seasoned Timber

Joseph Freda, *Suburban Guerrillas*

Ernest Hebert, *The Dogs of March*

Ernest Hebert, *Live Free or Die*

Kit Reed, *J. Eden*

Rowland E. Robinson (David Budbill, ed.),
Danvis Tales: Selected Stories

Roxana Robinson, *Summer Light*

Rebecca Rule, *The Best Revenge: Short Stories*

Theodore Weesner, *Novemberfest*

W. D. Wetherell, *The Wisest Man in America*

Edith Wharton (Barbara A. White, ed.),
Wharton's New England: Seven Stories and Ethan Frome

Thomas Williams, *The Hair of Harold Roux*

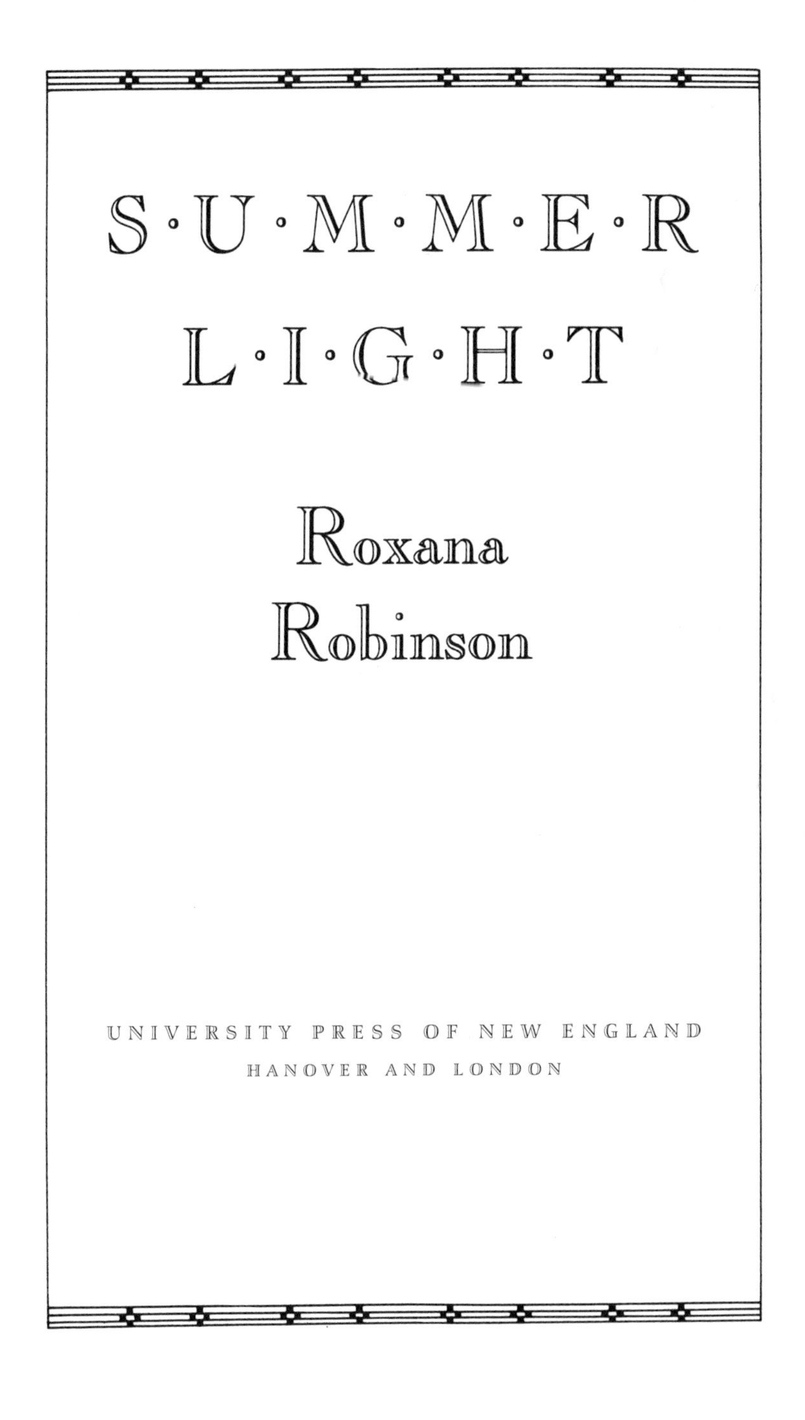

S·U·M·M·E·R L·I·G·H·T

Roxana Robinson

UNIVERSITY PRESS OF NEW ENGLAND
HANOVER AND LONDON

University Press of New England, Hanover, NH 03755

University Press of New England paperback edition published in 1995.
The novella *Summer Light* was first published, in a different form, in Great Britain by J. M. Dent & Sons Ltd. *Summer Light* was first published in hardcover by Viking Penguin in 1988, and simultaneously in Canada by Penguin Books Canada Ltd; and in paperback by Harper Perennial, a division of HarperCollins Publishers, in 1990.

Printed in the United States of America 5 4 3

Grateful acknowledgment is made for permission to reprint an excerpt from "Don't Stand So Close" by Sting.

LIBRARY OF CONGRESS CATALOGING IN PUBLICATION DATA
Robinson, Roxana.
Summer light / Roxana Robinson
p. cm. — (Hardscrabble books)
ISBN–0–87451–738–9 (alk. paper)
I. Title. II. Series
PS3568.03152S86 1995
813'.54—dc20 95–32560

To my mother,
Alice Scoville Barry,
as a small token
of the great tribute she deserves.

S·U·M·M·E·R L·I·G·H·T

One

It's much too foggy," Laura said flatly. "We can't go." She lay stretched out on a rumpled sofa near the window, her long legs, in faded jeans, blending with the scattered denim pillows. She pulled her long hair back from her face with both hands, and stared out of the window. Ordinarily, Great Cranberry Island could be seen clearly from the front porch of the old house they had rented in Northeast Harbor, but now she could barely see the porch railings: drifting swags of white obscured everything.

Ward, who lived with Laura, sat on the floor, playing Parcheesi with Sammy, Laura's four-year-old son. The two blond heads faced each other across the board, the two backs curved like parentheses around the game. Richie, who was married to Laura's sister, Sarah, sat in a threadbare armchair with the Sunday papers.

"It's barely foggy at all," Ward said, without looking up. "You just aren't wearing your glasses."

"Anyway it may clear by dinnertime," said Richie.

"Even if it hasn't cleared by then, it's a straight shot," said Ward. He moved a small red marker on the board. "Six, seven, eight. Gotcha," he told Sam. "It's a piece of cake. Due south out, due north back." Sam looked at the board, then—at the word *cake*—up at Ward. Ward smiled.

"But it will be different at night," argued Laura.

"No, it won't," Ward said. He turned to her. "Due south out, due north back. We have a compass."

"We'll be lost at sea," Laura pointed out. She saw them swept away in the darkness, a drifting point in a vast and hostile sea, far beyond help.

"No," said Ward, "we won't." Ward believed in facts, facts underlay his days and his transactions with the world.

Laura eyed him. She shoved up the sleeves of her purple sweater, revealing her thin pale arms. Laura felt that she spent her life listening to men who told her that things would work when she knew they would not: her vacuum cleaner, her carburetor, her marriage.

"We may as well go," said Richie. He wore round tortoise-shell glasses, and had high, rounded cheekbones and big teeth. He looked like a friendly Eskimo. He leaned back in his chair and stretched, his long arms in the ratty red sweater lifted high over his head. A bare patch of brown skin appeared across his stomach. As his head went back Laura saw on the top of it a thinning patch. This was a shock: she had not imagined Richie getting older. She looked away, as though she had seen something indecent.

Sarah stood up and began to stack dishes. "I think we should go," she said quietly; "we planned it." Sarah's own long, dark hair swung in a neat braid over her woven shirt, and she wore dark corduroy jeans and clogs. She moved calmly, with a sense of serene purpose. She was eight years older than Laura, and Laura thought she was perfect. At twenty-nine Laura at last preferred her own age to her sister's; still, she felt her sister's superiority to be deep and irreversible.

Sarah was always the first one to start working. Laura believed that there was some discrepancy between them, some early flaw in the casting, or in the metal itself. She believed that she would give off a tinselly clang if struck, compared to her sister's deep bell tone.

Their lives were very different. Sarah and Richie had done over an old farmhouse in the country, where she grew vegetables, made bread, knitted sweaters. Laura had never seen the house, but she imagined it set on a hillside, its white clapboards shining against the casual grass, its corners neat and firm, its fireplaces vast and comforting, its spaces welcoming. Laura longed, at times, to dissolve her own scratchy life in Sarah's, to give herself up to the circle of seasons, to the steady rise of yeast, the slow growth of woolen sleeves. Laura lived, uncertainly, in Ward's Central Park West apartment, not quite divorced from Sam's father, treading water, waiting for something that would set her life in order.

Laura sat up on the sofa and watched her sister, feeling, as always, rebuked by Sarah's industry.

Sarah finished loading the tray and carried it downstairs to the kitchen, humming. Laura stood up and stretched, now that Sarah had gone, and began to pick up the rest. Her own brown hair hung loose past her shoulders; her eyes were blue, not brown, and her nose was long and rather lordly. There was a resemblance between the two—clear, pale skin and high color, and a deceptive calmness about the eyes—but Sarah's face was round and her cheeks were full; she missed beauty by a narrow margin and Laura hit it sqaure. It was the beauty that confused Laura, that muddied her view. It held her like a vise, rigid in its grip. She was afraid to try to be anything else, afraid that that was all she was.

"What time will we have to leave?" Laura asked, and Sam looked up, now anxious.

"Leave where?" he asked, suspicious.

"We're going on a grown-up dinner," Laura said, putting the dishes down at once. "Come here." She held her arms out, but Sam, betrayed, would not go near her. She lunged, grabbed him and held him against her. The fire had suffused him with heat, and, holding him, Laura felt him warm and beloved next to her flesh. "You'd hate it," she said mendaciously, "and anyway you get to stay with Winifred." She spoke as though Winifred were a three-day trip to Hawaii, instead of their cheerful eighteen-year-old neighbor.

"Good deal, Sam," Ward said judiciously. "I wouldn't mind staying home with Winifred myself." He was putting the Parcheesi game away very neatly, each token going into a little slot. He looked up, to see how this had struck Sam. Ward, unlike the others, had pale caramel skin; he was half-Jewish, with a straight Roman nose, and thick loose rich curls—a dark grainy blond, the color of hay. Ward was big, and it seemed to Laura that his size, his solidity, must somehow connect him with the earth, the world, with those statements of facts, of absolutes, that men were so good at. Laura herself felt insubstantial in comparison, as though she might lose touch entirely at any moment.

Richie and Sarah's daughters, Pia and Karin, were at the movies, so Winifred and Sammy stood alone in the doorway, waving to them as they left. Winifred had blazing red hair, which was visible for a long time in the fog. Laura kept turning around to wave at Sammy, wondering if this would be the last time that he ever saw his mother. All of them wore long pants, heavy sweaters and slickers. Laura had tried to think of something she could produce triumphantly in case they were swept out to sea, but could think of nothing that would not be so obvious as to make her look ridiculous if they were not.

As they walked through the pine trees the dense fog cut them off from the known world. The trees seemed to solidify only just in time for them to pass by, and to begin dissolving a moment too soon.

Down at the dock, the boats leaned uncertainly in the mist, slipping quietly about in their stanchions. They climbed into their Boston whaler, cold and mist-filmed, and moved slowly past the other boats. The rest were deserted, the big yawls and ketches battened down against the weather.

Once out in the open water, Ward pushed forward on the throttle, and they began to ease quickly through the fog. Laura could hear the water lapping nearby, but she could not quite see it. The boat was all she could see, and past it and around it was the opalescent density of the fog. The sun irradiated it, shining into but not through it. There was a brilliance in the west.

By the time they reached Great Cranberry, it was nearly dark. The trip took forty minutes across the open water. As they approached the shoreline the fog thinned and lessened, and Laura watched lights appear through it, and boats, and the ghostly long, gray wooden dock where the ferry tied up and the little low building that was the restaurant.

Ward tied up the boat on the far side of the float, his blunt, thick fingers working surely among the heavy, stiff coils of rope. His hair stood up in spikes, salt-thickened, and his eyebrows were white with mist. He grinned at Laura, and put his arm around her as they walked along the dock.

"How was that?" he asked, squeezing her hand.

"Terrific," said Laura, reserving her real judgment. They were not home yet.

The restaurant was a pair of low-ceilinged rooms with a wall of windows overlooking the harbor. They were put in the small room; the big one was filled with people who would leave on the eight o'clock ferry. The waitress brought them drinks and, unexpectedly, hot popovers, which steamed damply when they were opened. The butter slid at once off their flabby yellow sides, melting into a rich, thick pool at their centers.

The first day, shopping together at the Pine Tree Market, Sarah had looked at the dense yellow blocks that Laura had put in the shopping cart.

"Oh, butter!" Sarah said, and, when Laura looked at her,

she went on. "I never buy it. We're all used to margarine and powdered milk." There were in her voice thin streaks of pride, self-righteousness, a conscious sense of virtue. Laura knew the tone: this was how they had grown up. Their lives had been governed by deliberate frugality, proof of their state of grace. It was not merely that they were poor—anyone might be poor—it was that they had *chosen* to be poor. Their father had converted to Quakerism, left his job at Morgan Stanley in Manhattan and moved the whole family down to Red Top, Maryland, to become the editor of the local paper. It was the triumph of principle over greed, and it had placed the whole family on a dais of pious superiority. They were superior, for example, to people who bought their clothes new: the fact that their own clothes were from the thrift shop, wrinkled and limp before the first wearing, made Laura's family more admirable.

Her father's strict and rigid moral vision had divided Laura's world into mutually exclusive parts; there was no overlapping, no shaded area, no forgiveness. Laura had always wished the division hadn't been so strict or so clear: beauty, plenty and sin on one side, dearth and virtue on the other. Early on, she had chosen the former, and now, as always, when faced with someone who had chosen the latter she was swept by exasperation, envy and helplessness.

"Want some butter?" Laura asked Sarah now, "or shall I see if they have any margarine?" She wished immediately that she had not said it.

But Sarah laughed, and said, "Don't bother. I'll make do with this stuff, whatever it turns out to be."

"Do you have a moral bias against butter?" asked Ward.

"Purely financial," said Sarah cheerfully.

"I support cows," said Richie. "I prefer a cow to a vegetable any day. I support the all-dairy spread."

"That sounds like a cattle ranch," Laura said.

But it was his fault, if it was anyone's, that they could not afford butter, she thought. Sarah had married Richie when he was at architecture school, and had struggled along, supporting them both with translating and typing jobs until he graduated. Richie's family was from New Canaan; he had grown up in a big white house overlooking the golf course. Laura had assumed that he would gradually become rich, drawing Sarah and their family into a creamy life, flowered towels in the guest room, girls' boarding schools, a kind black woman in the kitchen. Instead, he had taken her off to a tiny town in New Hampshire. They had a perilous existence in the old, cold farmhouse at the edge of a cow pasture. Richie designed houses (never the kind he wanted to) for a local developer, and the odd professional building for a mall. He had told Laura that he ran eighteen miles a day, and did most of his work at night. Laura had met him before Sarah had, the summer she was sixteen, and he was twenty-four. Laura had been in love with him.

"We support cats," announced Ward, "or some of us do." This was directed at Laura.

"Ward wants to kill my cat," she said, stirring things up.

"I don't recall saying that," said Ward.

"What is it that you want, then?"

"I want less cat pee," Ward said, making his hand into a fist and laying it gently down on the table, "that's what I want."

Laura's cat was a gray Maltese, shy, sweet, and very neurotic. Nathaniel, Laura's husband, had given Sheba to Laura as a wedding present, and Laura suspected that Ward disliked the cat for symbolic reasons. But Sheba was not a metaphor; she was a cat. She slept curled up in the crook of Laura's knee, and in the morning stood golden-eyed by Laura's face, purring in a steady rhythm of delight.

But in Northeast Harbor Sheba had sunk below the level of tolerable neurotics, even Laura admitted that. The cat was frightened of the three-story descent to the kitty litter in the laundry room, and she stayed in Laura and Ward's room, and made messes in the upper floors. She had peed on the bathroom rug and on one in the upstairs hall, and Laura had suspicions of the kindling box in the living room.

"She'll stop," said Laura. "She's just having a hard time settling down."

"If she doesn't stop, we're going to have to burn the house down to get rid of the smell," said Ward.

"But we won't have Sheba murdered," said Laura.

"Winifred tells me there's a very good ASPCA over in Manset," said Ward. "They're very careful about finding homes for animals."

"What is this, a conspiracy?" Laura asked. "You have a responsibility to your animals; you don't throw them out of your house just because they made a slip." She disliked the idea of Sheba in a cage, her plushy fur pressed against wire mesh, her golden eyes filled with dread: what of her own slips?

There was a pause, and Sarah sighed and shook her head. "Well, it is a problem," she said sympathetically. "Pets are supposed to give you pleasure, not misery. We had a cat called Scrubs. When he was about ten, he began to bite people. He bit everyone; he was like an attack cat. He bit us and the children. And then he started to pee on everything." She looked at Richie. "Remember, he peed all over the new suitcase you bought me. We had to throw it away."

"And what did you do with him?" asked Laura, sure it would be the right thing.

"Had him P.T.S.," said Richie.

"What's P.T.S.?" asked Ward.

"That's what it says on the ticket you get: 'Put To Sleep.' "

Ward began to laugh. "They give you a ticket for a dead cat? What do you do with that?"

9

But Laura was angry. How could Sarah have done this? "You really had him killed?"

"Actually, *I* had him killed," Richie said. "Your gentle lady sister *wanted* him killed, but she wouldn't soil her hands. She wouldn't even drive him to the vet's. I stood at the bottom of the stairs with poor old Scrubs in the traveling box, growling and spitting and trying to escape—as well he might—and I yelled upstairs, 'Governor Freeman! Governor Freeman! Governor Freeman! A last plea for clemency! The prisoner requests a pardon!' "

"And?" said Laura.

"She pretended she didn't hear me."

"I did not pretend," Sarah said. "I really didn't hear you."

"You really didn't want to answer," Richie said. "You wouldn't even tell the girls what you had done."

"I did too tell the girls."

"Finally."

For years, Laura had seen Sarah and Richie only at Christmas, in Maryland. They never came to New York, and Nat had always refused to make the long drive to their home in New Hampshire. ("It's ten hours, both ways," he would complain, "and, when we get there, we'll have to walk around in the mountains. And at dinner they'll have in Mormons for a sing-along.") But Laura had imagined Sarah and Richie happy in the countryside; she had imagined that they led a calm and unruffled life, that they never argued, that their gentleness extended to each other as well as to the rest of the world. Now she was embarrassed to hear them talking like this to each other, their sentences armed with sullen barbs.

"Oh, come on," Sarah said, smiling at Richie. "He had a very nice life."

"Up till then," Richie said. "He thought you were his friend. Up until then."

It was Ward who interceded. "But what would you have done with him?" he asked Richie.

Richie grinned. "Poor old Scrubs. I don't know. Probably the same thing. I just like to tease Madame Defarge here."

"There comes the waitress," said Laura, wanting a diversion.

They moved into the other room, which had emptied out. Most of the others had left on the ferry, and the people left were hardy types from the cruising sailboats moored in the harbor. Most of them were older, in their fifties and sixties, with ruddy faces. Men and women had short, graying hair, thick with the salt air, and they wore Shetland sweaters in heathery colors, and rubber-soled Topsiders. The room took on a quiet air of clubbishness; everyone was pleased with himself at being there in spite of the treachery of the surrounding night.

Cheered by the change in atmosphere and by the arrival of dinner, they all smiled at each other, sat up straighter, expanded.

"How's your photography?" Sarah asked Laura.

This question filled Laura with anxious lethargy, always. The idea of an answer seemed impossible. Her voice would drop to a boring drone; she would lose track of the words she meant to use; she would flounder. Once she had forgotten the word "print."

"Fine," she said, her eyes glazing over.

"Anything new going on? What are you working on now?"

"Anything new going on" meant "Are you going to have a show?" or "Have you published anything?" Before she had left Nat, photography had been the source of Laura's greatest and most private bliss. Even when she had stopped for weeks, as she had when Sammy was born, she had felt it waiting—secret, absorbing—for her to take it up again. Now, with all her convictions challenged, she wavered horribly. She was poisoned by the fear that what she did was worthless, useless. She had not worked at all since she had quit her job.

"Nothing new," she said, arranging her wine and water glasses on the table. "I did a series of masks, actually."

"Masks?" asked Sarah encouragingly.

"Yes," said Laura. She could not go on.

"Why do you take photographs, anyway? Would you tell our audience?" Richie held out his fist for her to talk into, his voice full of synthetic interest.

"To get rich, of course," Laura said blandly. "That's my only reason. Tell our audience why you run," she said.

"It's faster," said Richie.

"That's not an answer," said Laura.

"Neither was yours," said Richie, smiling at her.

Ward put his arm around Laura, draining off her tension like a lightning rod. "Why do you keep cats?" he asked.

Laura began to laugh, and leaned her head against Ward's arm. It was terribly warm; she could feel the heat from it flooding through her.

Sarah smiled, and stretched her arms over her head. "This is fun," she said; "this was a great idea, Ward."

Laura was pleased she had said "Ward" instead of Laura. "Let's do it again next year," she said.

Everyone laughed. "We're only three days into it," cautioned Ward. "We might end up not speaking to each other."

The fog was pressing against the building, and the windowpanes looked as though they had been roughly painted out. Laura squinted myopically at them, and Richie noticed.

"Are you composing a picture?" he asked.

"I don't compose them," she answered; "they're already there. The best ones are sometimes in the beginning of the roll that I snap just to get it going."

"My favorite picture is the one you took at Inchfawn of your granny."

Inchfawn had been Laura and Sarah's grandmother's house in Bar Harbor, a vast, shingled warren of dim rooms. Laura had taken a photograph of her standing on the porch that stretched the length of the house, high-ceilinged and shadowy. Granny stood small and fierce at the top of the porch steps, dominating the huge house behind her. She had died three years after Laura took the picture. The girls' parents had hesitated about the house: by that time Bar Harbor was no longer fashionable. Most of the big houses had burned down in the great fire during the forties, and Inchfawn was then in a rather seedy area. During the spring of their hesitation the house burned to the ground—the big sweet-smelling linen closets, the dusty box-rooms, the sleeping porches, the painted beds, the filmy curtains, the wicker furniture along the porch, all gone for good.

"I took that the first summer I ever took pictures," said Laura. It had been the summer she had met Richie, when she was staying with her grandmother alone for the first time, before Sarah had arrived. It was a strong photograph—an accident, partly the angle, partly the northern light, for Laura knew nothing about photography then. She had given a print of it to Richie and Sarah as a wedding present: it was the house where, and the summer, they met.

"Are you going to keep your cat?" Ward asked suddenly.

"What do you want? You want her P.T.S., don't you?"

"I want you to marry me," said Ward, and Laura began to laugh. It was not the first time he had said that, in a mild, uninsistent and inappropriate way. She had not yet answered him; the question frightened her. It was not that she did not want to be married: being a divorced mother seemed somehow shameful to her. What held her back was the fear that she would fail at this one too. Laura saw herself defined by failure, like the bright outline around a Matisse figure.

After they had coffee, they put on their sweaters and went out into the dark. The waitress called out, "Good luck!" as the door closed behind them, and they stepped out into the night, adventurous, filled with admiration for themselves. In the dark they lowered their voices. There were no lights now along the rickety pier, and the narrow shaft of the flashlight did not seem big enough for the whole black night. Everything seemed magnified in the dark. The boat was more precarious, the waves more haphazard. The seats were drenched, and the cold dampness began to seep immediately into Laura's legs. That was something I could have brought, she thought; just a square plastic bag, to sit on. They started out cautiously. They had a chart and a compass, but no running lights, only the small flashlight. The boat moved away from the few lights on the island. Ahead, nothing was visible. Ward began to talk about how easy it was going to be.

"Due north," he said. "We can't miss. We're practically surrounded by land, anyhow. In almost any direction we'll hit land."

"What if we do hit land?" asked Laura. "What if we run into Sutton Island?"

"If we run into Sutton Island at this speed," said Ward, "we'll put her into reverse and back very carefully away, and we'll all promise never to mention it to anyone."

"How will you know which way to turn?" persisted Laura. I mean, how will you know it's Sutton and not Mount Desert?"

"I have special ways of knowing," said Ward. He had grown up with boats; he had worked in a marina when he was in college. He was steering, and Richie was holding the flashlight, standing next to him. The beam of light alternated between the compass and the darkness ahead of them. Laura could see nothing, even with the flashlight, and she watched the narrow ray of light that reflected off the fog and threw up huge shadows that looked like island shapes looming over her.

"North, north," said Richie. "We're ten degrees off."

"Right," said Ward, and brought the helm around. Once they were a hundred and ten degrees off, because Ward had been looking at what he thought was a boat. Laura had not felt the boat turn off its course. The rest of them stopped talking after that, except for Ward.

"Full speed ahead!" he announced cheerfully.

"Don't!" said Laura, stretched by tension.

"I *won't,*" said Ward. They were crawling through the night. He began to sing "Nearer My God to Thee." Richie laughed and joined in. They sang it for hours, it seemed, making up verses about those in peril on the sea. Finally they stopped. Ward cut the engine to listen. They had been traveling for most of the night, Laura thought.

"We'll listen for a moment," said Ward. "We'll listen for the gong." He turned the flashlight off and the dark closed in like ether around them. They sat rocking and silent in the black fog. Laura leaned forward in her seat, concentrating so hard on seeing and hearing that those two senses vanished altogether. She felt the boat begin to tip forward; she felt the plane of the sea begin to tilt. She saw little jittery bright flashes, like the specks in an old movie.

Sarah was sitting next to Laura, and Laura felt her shiver. "Are you cold?" Laura asked, and Sarah nodded. She wrapped her parka around Sarah and herself, like a cocoon. Still, even pressed against Sarah and hearing her breathe, she could not make things be normal.

She thought of being home, she thought of Sam, and of going upstairs to kiss him good night. She thought of Ward telling her, as he always did, not to worry. She could hear nothing, there was no sound around them except for the small, incessant slap of invisible water against the boat. Ward turned on the engine again and started off, and Laura felt them all hurtling blind through the night.

"This is terrific," said Ward. "What an adventure!"

Laura turned to look at him. He was standing very straight, squinting into the dark. When he saw her face, he grinned. Laura wondered if he were drunk. She was tired and anxious and cold. She did not think they were having a wonderful adventure.

"Listen," said Richie, "there's a bell."

They all froze. Richie was right: they all heard a low, clear tone coming from out of the gloom.

"You're right," said Ward, "let's have a look at the chart."

They bent over the chart with the flashlight, but it was not all right. They were not, as it turned out, supposed to hear a bell. There was no bell near their course.

"There's one over here," said Richie. "Do you think that's where we are?"

"If that's where we are, then we're slowly sinking," said Ward. "It's right on top of the ledge." There was a pause. "That can't be right." The bell tolled unevenly, tipped by the waves. "Look at this," said Ward. "There's a bell just off the lighthouse, at the edge of the harbor. There's the bell right there. That's where we must be."

"If we're right by the lighthouse, why can't we see it?" asked Richie. "Why can't we see the light?"

According to the chart, the Bear Island Lighthouse sends, every six seconds, a beam of light that can be seen for seventeen miles, alerting mariners to the treacherous shoals and granite ledges that lie off Mount Desert Island and the surrounding islands. Passing fifty feet from its bell, as they seemed to be, even blindfolded they should have sensed the sweep, felt the sudden irradiation of the fog. Laura strained, watching for the broad, ghostly beam that would drench her, leave her. There was nothing.

"I think we're over here," said Richie, pointing to the first bell. "Nowhere near the lighthouse."

"We can't be," Ward said flatly. "We've been going due north the whole time."

What about the time we were a hundred and ten degrees off, thought Laura, what if something else went wrong, that we didn't discover? How could Ward be so sure, in the black of night, of where he was?

There was a pause. Laura thought of the fire in the living room. They had been going nearly an hour in some direction through the bleak dark.

Richie spoke, and his voice held all the thoughts that lay in Laura's mind, all the possibilities that surrounded them in an open boat in perilous seas.

"I don't know," he said. "Let's just go over and look at the bell. Once we see its number, we'll know exactly where we are."

This made sense to Laura: the sound was the only contact they had with reality. It promised a solid object, one that would correspond with a real, known place on the chart; one that would link their own theoretical existence with a specific location in the world. She felt they might stay lost forever; they might continue on and on through the blank, baffling night, watching and watching and watching.

"I agree with Richie," she said. Why had they come out into the night at all? Why were they not in front of the fire, finishing a second bottle of wine?

Ward was irritated at her mutinous support of Richie. "Now, look," he said, "I am at the helm."

In the fog, the dense mountainous shadows looming over them, Laura thought of Sammy; she ached for Sammy. She wanted to fold him in her arms and shut out the rest. She couldn't bear Ward; the fact that he drew breath in her presence oppressed her. Why had she allowed him into her house, her life, her family?

"If we went over to that bell," said Ward, "close enough to see which one it is, we'll know exactly where we are. We'll be right exactly on top of Seal Ledge, that's where we'll be.

Even if it were high tide, which it isn't, there would be only six inches of water on some of those rocks. It's close to low tide now, and even though some of them would be out of the water, in this fog and in the dark we wouldn't see them until we'd hit them." No one spoke. The water made light slaps against the boat. "We're going due north."

Laura hated Ward with a passion. He was so bossy; he was imperious and arrogant. Why was she not spending her life with someone like Richie, who recognized that there were things like fear and indecision, who saw life as something to be encountered and considered and adapted to, not as something to be hacked and chopped and split into your own idea of a landscape? She had chosen wrong again.

She sat next to Sarah, her arm warm from her sister's.

"I can't stand Ward," she whispered to Sarah, as though she were making a pledge.

Ward started the engine again and the boat moved off sluggishly. Ward was no longer grinning. He was standing very straight and staring into the fog. Laura felt the boat pound along through the night, and the sound of the engine and the sound of her blood roared in her ears. Sarah leaned toward her and said softly, beneath the sound of the engine, "There *isn't* any way we could be going out to sea, is there?"

Much as Laura wanted to criticize Ward, to condemn his cold-blooded imperiousness, she wanted even more to reassure her sister. She wanted Sarah calm and happy. "No," she said with great certainty. "We're going due north, right into the harbor. Ward's right." She looked back at Ward, who gave a solemn wink, as though they were allies, as though they were great friends. The mournful eyes, the long, sad nose, were transformed by this secret promise, this reassurance that they were allies, that they were great friends, and lovers. Laura smiled at him in spite of herself. She felt the steadiness of their course against the tide, against the shifting waves, against the muffling blanket of fog. She could feel Ward's purpose, and his certainty began to creep into her.

She stared into the night, and thought she saw a whiteness. It vanished when she looked at it, but when she glanced sideways, tricking it, it reappeared. "Look!" she said. They all saw it. They turned off the flashlight and watched. It stayed, a shimmer moving slowly toward them. It was a miracle.

"There you are," said Ward. "It's the Burdens' dock. Right on target."

Richie began to laugh. "It is, goddamnit!' Relief streamed through his voice. "Right on the button! Christmas!"

As they neared Clifton Dock, farther in the harbor, things appeared. The world of objects emerged casually, unremarkably. The air cleared; the fog thinned and lessened. Laura found her legs and arms to be stiff, as though they had been tightly clenched for forty minutes in the night air. She shook one arm and stretched, shaking from her the muffling tension of the fog. She felt lightheaded, and smiled largely at Sarah, as though she herself had just performed some clever trick. She turned to Ward, who looked pleased.

"There we are," he said, bringing the boat into the slip. "Did you doubt for an instant?"

"Not for an instant," said Laura, renouncing the pledge she had made to Sarah. Ward had, after all, brought her home.

Still, when they went to bed, offended that he had been right about everything, she kept her distance. She turned her back to him, standing in front of the open window as she pulled off her sweater. "I'm freezing," she announced, and put on a long nightgown. She slid into bed, without looking at him.

"Why have you got that thing on?" Ward asked, sliding his hand under her hips and pulling her over to him.

"Ward, you're such a bully," Laura said crossly.

"Yeah," said Ward, moving his hand along her leg. "You have a rotten life. Imagine living with a man like me."

"I mean it," Laura said. "You want to run everything."

"Okay, we'll switch. Tomorrow you run everything."

Laura began to laugh. "Ward," she said.

"Why do you have this thing on? Take it off," he said. His hand slid up inside it. "No, on second thought, leave it on," he said; "it's kind of kinky."

Two

The day after the boat trip was overcast, the air was damp and uninviting. Laura stood in her underpants on the braided rug and pulled on a pair of pink jeans. She stared down at them.

"Ward, are these too wrinkled?" she asked.

"I thought they were supposed to be, right at the tip," he said, reaching out and touching a nipple. "They feel nice, anyway," he said encouragingly. "No one will notice." He went downstairs.

Laura pulled on a T-shirt and went up to find Sam, who was damp and grubby and cheerful, deeply absorbed in the Lego on his bed.

"Aha," said Laura. This was a set piece.

"Aha," said Sam, preoccupied.

"A mouselet," said Laura.

"A mommy," said Sam, as planned. "But Mommy," he went on, looking up, "I am not your mouselet."

This was new. Interested, Laura sat down beside him.

"You're not?" she asked.

"No," said Sam firmly, fitting together a wheel and an axle. "I am your son."

Laura fell over sideways on the bed, closing her eyes in an expression of extreme desolation. "I don't have a mouselet anymore," she breathed, as though dying.

Sammy looked over at her and smiled, delighted at his power. "I'm sorry, Mommy," he said, falsely kind, "you'll just have to make the best of things." He tried, not hard, to keep from smiling. Laura lay still. He patted her on the shoulder. "Cheer up, Mommy," he said. "Be brave."

Laura sat up and sighed. "Is that what I have to do?"

Sam nodded. "Be brave, Mommy," he said, as she had said to him thousands of times, devaluing his pain, misery, humiliation. Children are so powerless, she thought, watching him; it's so unfair. She drooped her head, and Sam patted her gently on the knee, compassionate, insincere. "It will be all right."

Laura acted a slow recovery. "I hope so," she said, and began unbuttoning his pajamas, feeling the heat from his damp, smooth skin.

"Sambo, what do you think of Maine? Do you like it? Isn't it neat?"

"Yes," said Sam. "Do we live here now?"

"No," said Laura, pained. "We live in New York. This is only for a month in the summer. Then we'll go back to our apartment in New York."

Of course she meant Ward's apartment: she and Sammy had none.

When Laura had split up with Nat, she and Sammy had stayed on in their apartment until it was sold, and then she had taken over a lease in Soho. She had thought Soho would be a new life for her—clean, white walls, big spaces, fresh minds. She had been miserable there.

Laura worked for a magazine uptown, and at night she would struggle up the ringing iron stairs of her building and stand on the cavernous landing, groceries in her arms, fumbling with her heavy keys, her toes curling inside her boots to keep warm; hoping that the babysitter had been kind and diligent and that she had not been robbed again. She had been robbed three times that winter; there was no elevator in her building, the heat was grudging and sporadic.

She did not feel, after all, that she belonged in Soho. She did not fit in with these strange, boisterous people in their baggy, gloomy terrorist clothes. She did not dare call herself a photographer, down there: there were photographers in Soho who took pictures of things she could not even consider—rock stars naked, red fish, harsh flowers—vivid, wild things.

There were no supermarkets, and no children. Laura pushed Sammy's stroller over the bumpy cobblestones to distant, tiny parks smelling of dogshit. Her housekeeper had quit, and she had to make do with slovenly, reluctant babysitters who spoke no known language. The last was a cheerful young woman from Russia with bright pink cheeks. She was shaped like a dome on the Kremlin, and in English could only say "Denkyou." Laura came home late one night to find that Elena had left on time. Sammy was alone on the floor with his toys, cheerful and placid. Laura was enraged. She called Elena and tried to inform her that she was fired. "Denkyou," Elena said.

The lease was up in mid-February. Ward had said, "Move in with me. All mod cons, twenty-four-hour doorman, great sex."

"With the doorman?" Laura had asked, but she meant "Fine." She had sent all her own furniture into storage and moved in. The apartment was perfect for Sammy—big, with wide halls and large rooms, space and comfort. There was a nursery school three blocks away. The doorman was a handsome, straight-backed Puerto Rican named Harold, who helped Laura with the stroller, and signaled for taxis with an authoritative blast from a big silver whistle. It was a great relief. What she wanted for Sammy was a sense of place, of certainty.

Still, when she had wheeled him across the threshold of the apartment and told him, "This is where we're going to live," her heart had sunk. She was in another man's house. What was she doing there? She remembered, in a book about a murderer, the girl who had been in the car with her boyfriend and two small children. After an argument the girl had stepped from the car with her children and stood teetering on the narrow strip of concrete divider, waiting for someone else to come along and pick them up. Laura was afraid she was losing control of her life. Ward's apartment was peaceful and secure after the chaos of Soho, but what if things didn't work out with Ward? How many times could she say to Sammy, this is where we're going to live, this is who I love?

Laura was assistant photography editor on a fashion magazine. She had been there for three years; she had gotten the job through her photography teacher at the School of Visual Arts. "It's who you know," he had told Laura. "Also the publisher is a leg man. That won't hurt you." Laura had gone in for the interview and been shown in to the editor's office, Justine. Justine was tall, white-faced, bony and glamorous, and she liked dramatic gestures. She smoked with a water filter, and waved it in the air while she talked. She had a smoker's voice, deep and roughened, and wore tight, black cashmere and loose ivory bangles. She waved her cigarette holder at Laura, nodded violently, her eyes shut, and pointed at a chair in front of the desk. She was on the telephone to a friend: she was trying to rent her house for the month of July, Laura discovered.

"It's *actually* in the Springs," Justine drawled, "but it *feels* like Southhampton, and it's really decorated that way, I mean . . . Oh, you're sweet to say that; it's not *fancy* at *all,* you know it's just a lot of nonsense, there isn't a *serious* piece of furniture in the whole place . . . Oh, you're sweet to say that, of course *your* house is di*vine*, I mean mine is really a sort of shepherd's *cot*tage next to yours, but that's sort of what I was *after* . . ." She nodded suddenly at Laura, as though she had just seen her, and waved her hand ambiguously at the telephone. Laura smiled politely, her feet crossed neatly at the ankles, and waited.

She would not have taken the job if it had not been for Marina, the photography editor. Marina was clever and plain and chic, with thick, black hair pulled tighty away from her face, big earrings, bulgy eyes and a wide mouth. She was direct and kind and decisive, and she protected Laura from the other editors, and their roil of competitive dressing and talking. Laura was always faintly tousled, making it clear that she was not in the competition. Her long hair was always loose, and there was always, somewhere, a row of swinging fringe, a knotted sash, something unsecured. She did not dare to present herself as finished, as though this was the best she could do. Laura loved the glitter, the action, the excitement of her job; the scorn and bitchiness alarmed her. She was fascinated and unnerved by the other editors; they seemed like serpents, brilliant and deadly.

Six months after she had moved in with Ward, Marina called her into her office and shut the door.

"Do you want some coffee?" she asked. "It's hit the fan."

"What do you mean?" Laura asked, thinking that whatever the problem was, it would be one that she would face with Marina.

"Larry met some new woman at a sex weekend. He's going to make her editor-in-chief. We're all in trouble."

"You're not serious," said Laura. This was, after all, a national magazine. The publisher, Larry, was famous for priapism, but he had never been quite so blatant about using it as a hiring technique. "Anyway, what do you mean, a sex weekend?"

"I mean a weekend retreat, like an encounter weekend. Sponsored by some porn group, I don't know. Anyway, she's done something to poor old Larry. Justine told me about it; she's already looking for something else. So am I. You can stay here and try for my job, if you like. I'll help you if I can. Or you can start looking yourself."

Laura could not believe her. There was Marina's office, after all, unchanged: the pale-pink walls covered with photographs for the fall issues; the sleek, silver slatted blinds at the window; Marina's glowing paperweight on her desk, an underwater fantasy of brilliant chips and petals; her porcelain coffee mug. Nothing had changed.

But the next week she had seen Larry showing a short, blond woman with sleepy eyes and big lips around the office. Laura saw with distress how cozy they were together, how closely they walked through the halls, their bodies casually touching in an unprofessional way. Marina had been told without explanation that she would not be going on a shooting trip she had planned. She had already booked the models, the plane tickets, the photographer; she had already chosen and packed the clothes they were to shoot. When Marina told Laura that, her paperweight was gone from her desk. Laura looked around for it but did not want to ask. Marina was gone in a week.

Laura vacillated; she had an insubstantial talk with Larry, who introduced her to the infamous Joyce. They talked vaguely about responsibilities, and said they hoped that Laura would be able to assume them. The responsibilities were not defined, and Laura could see she would not be offered Marina's job; they were just using her as a temporary stopgap while they found another photography editor. Laura wondered where they were looking—more sex weekends? She knew she should take a stand but could not bring herself to. She was not, secretly, sure that she could be photography editor on her own. She liked having Marina in charge. Marina was definite, with a point of view. Laura had a point of view, but she was not sure she could manage the rest of it: the sulky, vapid models; the prima donna photographers trying to get in a little sex on the side; drugs; missed planes; lost reservations. She liked having Marina make the decisions, form the center of things.

One day Joyce had called her in to her office, which she had painted a deadly acid green. Joyce spoke without moving her big lips, and without looking at Laura. Laura could see that she had been hopelessly tainted by Marina, that she was perceived as being Old Guard. They would not give her Marina's job no matter what she did.

Joyce had held up a set of photographs that Laura had taken—winter clothes, big bulky sweaters, thick jackets, knitted coats.

"I hate these pictures," Joyce said, not looking at Laura. It was a difficult beginning.

"The clothes?" Laura asked hopefully.

"The *pic*tures," Joyce said, holding them up above her in the air and studying them as though to steep herself in antipathy.

"I'm sorry," Laura began and instantly regretted it: it wasn't her fault Joyce hated the pictures. The clothes were terrible. One of the fashion editors had chosen them, reluctantly, because the manufacturer had taken four full-color pages every month for the last year. They were horrible clothes and made the models, thin as they were, look like stuffed geese.

"Well," Joyce cut in. She shook her head and looked extremely irritated, pursing her mouth and raising the outer edges of her eyebrows. "I just hate them. We have to project an *image* in this magazine; I don't know if you're aware of that. I'm not going to *fire* you over this, but I want to remind you that we can't have this sort of thing in the magazine. This is a *fashion* magazine, you know; we have to keep that in mind." She still did not look at Laura.

Not going to fire her over that set of pictures? Laura stared at Joyce. She might as well fire her because the elevators were all full at lunchtime. She could see that Joyce wanted very badly to fire her: what were her chances?

"I quit," she said experimentally, to see how it sounded. Joyce looked at her for the first time, and, pleased, Laura said it louder, and went back to clean out her desk.

"Good," Ward told her at home, putting his arm around her. "There was no hope under that witch, anyway. She's just jealous because you're better in bed than she is. Now you can do your own work. You did the right thing."

For Sammy, it had seemed like the right thing. He had begun, in the months while they had been living with Ward, to resist her departures in the mornings. Each day as she walked toward the front door, having kissed him goodbye, he would follow her, throwing his arms around her legs. "Mommy!" he would shout. "Please don't leave me! Please *don't!*" Laura would gently disentangle his arms; she would crouch down to his level and reason with him. She would remind him of his trip to the park with Erendina, their new housekeeper. She would remind him of his lunch, his toys, but she knew she was being false, prevaricant, to his luminous, devastating honesty. What he was saying was, How can you prefer to spend the day without me? You are my whole world, how can I not be yours? Instead of answering this question—how could she?—she was trying shamelessly to distract him, confuse him, muddy the issue, as you would try to do with a person you didn't like. Often Sam refused to be distracted, clinging still to her stockinged legs and ignoring her talk about parks and lunch. He would return to his anguish, to the question: would she stay with him? Then Laura would call for Erendina, who would come smiling from the kitchen and seize Sammy from behind and carry him off. Laura would open the heavy front door and close it behind her, but she could still hear Sammy's crying. Even in the elevator, as it plunged her down toward the strict geometry of the street—the grown-up, outside world—she could hear Sammy's sad calls.

When she quit her job, it was at first a relief. She planned to take some photography courses, do some work on her own and spend time with Sam. She took him herself to the park, she gave him baths, she reassured him that he was at the center of her world. When he started nursery school in the fall, it was Laura who took him, she who collected him. She loved waiting at the steps, with all the mothers milling expectantly, their faces turned peacefully toward the door, waiting for their small, cherished packages, watching for the first small figure to appear, shambling raggedly after the teacher, rumpled and flyaway, utterly trusting.

At home, she sat in the kitchen, reading to him while he worked his way through his sandwich. He ate noisily, his throat chugging steadily as he drank his milk, but he listened with absolute concentration, his mouth hanging open, absorbed, when she described the girl Lucy finding a fawn beneath a streetlamp in the woods.

Later, after his nap, she took him to the park. Slowly, they rumbled the Big Wheel across the sidewalk, its churning roar announcing Sam's importance in the world. Ward lived on Seventy-third Street. In that neighborhood there were few mothers in the park, it was mostly nannies. These grouped together in terms of ethnic origin: none were white Americans, and Laura usually sat alone. She brought a book, but it was difficult to concentrate: the shrill cries from the playground all sounded alike, and any one of them might mean it was Sam pounding his transformer against someone else's temple, or someone pounding against Sam's temple. Usually she sat aimlessly, watching, thinking about nothing.

Since she had quit her job Sam had visibly calmed. He played more quietly in the park, was not so raucous and destructive; he had lost that wild, sidelong, defiant glance. And he fell asleep, now, without first appearing forlornly in the doorway of her bedroom to see if she was still there. He no longer cried each time she and Ward went out to dinner.

Still, gloom began to settle around Laura. There were days when she could hardly face the elevator man, when she could not make up a face, a being, a sentence to present to the world, to convince it of her existence. There were days, that winter and spring, when she would take Sammy to nursery school and come back to lie heavily on her unmade bed in the darkened bedroom until it was time to pick him up again. There were days when she felt the world around her to be fashioned of some inalterable substance, something hard and brilliant. She felt herself insubstantial in this landscape. The lists of her failures occupied her consciousness, all the stupid, unkind mistakes she had ever made were vividly alive in her head.

In the newspapers she read about toxic wastes. At night she thought about poisons leaching slowly through the earth, and in the daylight she felt as though the air she moved through was filled with radiant death. She was surrounded by a fine, terrible tension; she could hardly breathe. She took no pictures.

She hoped she was in love with Ward. She wanted so much to be, that she did not trust herself. She wished she had no choice—a hundred years ago she would have married a good father to her son, romantic aspirations aside. But this was now, and, besides, it was hardly fair to Ward, to marry him for Sammy's sake: that was not, she knew, the way he saw it. She did not trust herself, and she did not believe she had the right to make choices, changes. She knew no way to resolve her muddle, and she was afraid that Ward would resolve it all by leaving her.

The month in Maine was meant as a cure. The empty air, the blue distances overhead, everything wild, unknown, fresh—

it was supposed to be a month of sustenance and calm. So far, the gentle ocean air had not closed around her with the threat of tension, and she felt removed from the dangerous reverberations of the city. Sammy's question reminded her, and she smoothed his head with calming strokes, as though it were he who was anxious. "You know where we live," she told Sam gently. "In September you'll go back to school, and maybe you'll get Miss Jacobs again." She wanted him to believe he had a home, though she did not.

Downstairs, Ward had made coffee and was reading the paper. Laura considered his face for a photograph, surprising herself; she never took pictures of people she knew. Her last project—masks—had been of strangers whose faces were concealed by hats, sunglasses, shadows. That had been months ago. Now she cocked her head: Ward's eyebrows arched away from the steam rising out of the mug, and his shirt was open at his big throat.

Laura liked the different textures, the airy cloud of steam, the glasses he wore for reading faintly misting, the faint glimmer of gold hair at his throat, the thick, blue flannel shirt and the hieroglyphic black and white of the newspaper. His face, as he looked up at her, was open, his eyes warm.

Laura started fixing breakfast for herself and Sam; Sarah and her daughters came in. Pia and Karin were twelve and fifteen, and looked very similar, with long, blond hair, long, brown legs, clear skin and white teeth. But Pia was still a girl and had not yet crossed the terrible bridge separating adolecence from childhood.

Karin, dramatically, had. Karin slammed doors; she swore loudly; she refused to wash her feet, brush her teeth or take part in any of the other ceremonies of civilization. For some reason she was a throwback to the sixties, though she had been born at the very end of the decade. She wore her hair in a snarly cascade down her back, and a tattered, voluminous skirt to her ankles.

"Here's breakfast," said Sarah, putting scrambled eggs on the table.

"I don't want any of this shit," said Karin, pushing a plate farther away from her. Laura stared at her. Sarah picked up the plate and put it next to Pia. Ward did not look up. Sammy laid his fork down and watched Karin, who picked up a skinny braid that hung down next to her temple. Richie appeared.

"Hello," he said. "Hello, hello, hello, hello," going around the table. Karin did not look up. "Hello, my little chickadee," he said to her. "Are we going hiking today?"

Karin looked up, her face transformed. "Oh, goody," she said; "with a picnic?"

"A Picnic!' Richie said, speaking the word so they could all see what he meant by it: ruby-colored grapes, creamy cheeses, crusty loaves, sumptuous cakes.

"A picnic!" echoed Sammy.

"Not us," said Laura quickly. She had had enough togetherness the night before. "Ward's leaving today, and you and I are going to drive him to the airport."

"I can get a car to pick me up," began Ward, but Laura shook her head at him.

"A hike means a real hike, a long one," she told Sammy, "and no one will carry you. If you come with me, we'll stop at the bumper cars on the way home." Threats and bribes, thought Laura, the real backbone of child-raising.

Pia helped Laura and Sarah with the dishes. Karin went out and sat on the porch in a rocking chair, looking like a dirty stork.

"Ma, why is Karin so horrible?" Pia asked.

"Now, Pia," Sarah said, smiling into space. "Karin is feeling very unsure of herself right now. She's not a grown-up and she's not a child."

"She's a pig," said Pia. Laura laughed. Sarah did not. Laura sank her hands into the dishwater, feeling for the hard, smooth china curves beneath the suds. Sarah took up a dish towel and began to dry. Karin appeared in the doorway, a radio pressed to her ear.

"I love this song," she said, "it is so *ex*cellent." She grinned at Sarah, listening, and Laura thought of another photograph: the narrow braid arching past her cheek, her eyes heavily focused, her mouth intent—partly opened in a faint smile—the heavy fall of hair onto her shoulders. She closed her eyes. Her smooth, fresh skin was no coarser than Sammy's, but her expression was one of passionate abandon. "I love you baby," she crooned, her eyes closed. Suddenly they opened, and she focused on her mother. "*Ma,*" she said, outrage in her voice, "*why* are you *doing* that? I'll dry the dishes, and you sit and drink your coffee or whatever that disgusting stuff is that you drink."

Karin vibrated with frantic, restless energy; you could feel it across the room, thought Laura, sex, mostly: Karin was wearing a soft, tight T-shirt and no bra. Her flattish, jiggly breasts, with little pointy tips like ice-cream cones, pressed against the thin fabric. She must feel wild, thought Laura, all that brand-new equipment and nothing to use it on.

Laura slid a glass around in her hands, feeling it turn glossy under the scalding rinse water. She wondered if Sammy, in adolescence, would turn on her a beam of dazzling insolence. It seemed unfair, to raise a friend and watch him become your enemy. But adolescence is pure enmity, she thought. She wondered if Sammy would choose to go and live with his father. She had read somewhere that Jesuit priests, expecting torture in Protestant Tudor England, had prepared for it simply by thinking about it, by acknowledging its presence as a probability in their lives. Know the risks, she warned herself; be ready.

The picnickers left before Ward had to go to the airport, the hamper and the children in the back seat, Pia waving vaguely as the car vanished among the pines. Laura went back downstairs to sit with Ward. They moved out onto the porch with their coffee, and Sam began an elaborate construction with the Lego among the legs of the wicker rocking chairs.

"Well," said Laura, "what do you think?"

"About your family?"

Laura nodded, sitting cross-legged on her chair. Below, the channel spread even and mild before them, ingenuous, shivering with light. It was impossible to imagine it as it had been the night before—dense, implacably shrouded. Laura took a sip of her coffee and looked at Ward, waiting.

"Nice," Ward said, smiling at her. "I like them. Karin's a bit of a time bomb, isn't she?"

Laura nodded, grinning. "I'm glad I'm not Sarah."

"What would you do?"

"God knows. Though I suppose parents of teenagers are always the worst-suited people for the job. Mine were."

"I thought you liked your parents."

Laura waved her hand, exasperated. "Oh, I liked my parents, everyone liked my parents; my parents are wonderful. That's the trouble; they're so principled. They make me feel like the whore of Babylon."

"What, because you're living in sin with me?"

"More that I'm getting a divorce, and that I buy expensive clothes and like to lie on the beach."

Ward smiled at her. "Oh, well, that makes sense. But what about being a good mother, don't you get marks for that?"

Laura shook her head. "That goes without saying." She yawned, shut her eyes and dug her knuckles deep into the sockets. The light flared and vanished behind her eyelids.

"It sounds as if you don't get marks for anything."

Laura shrugged. "It's a pain, having your parents be so good. It means you can't rebel without being a real shit. You're supposed to be idealistic and high-minded when you rebel from your parents: we could only be selfish and materialistic. And for the rest of your life, every time you do something good, you wonder if you really feel like doing it, or if you're still just trying to please your parents."

"But did you try to please your parents?"

Laura smiled at him. "Well, I wasn't unnatural. All little kids want to please their parents. But I went over to the devil, early on. As soon as I could talk, I started fighting with my mother about what I would wear. Every morning my mother would try to put me in overalls, and every morning I would hold out for a dress. I hated overalls; they made me feel as though I'd died. They were baggy, they were made for boys, and I felt as if I were wearing a pair of mail sacks."

"So, what happened?"

"Every day my mother would start to look sad and worn down and defeated. Part of me would think, How horrible you are to your mother; look how you're hurting her; why don't you give in and wear the overalls? And another part of me would shriek, Wear the dress! Go for the ruffles! Have a waist!"

"And who would win?"

Laura tapped herself on the chest. "Heartless, here, every day."

Ward rocked back and forth. "I wouldn't exactly call you heartless," he said judiciously. He smiled at her, and pushed the rocker back until his weight was on the outermost tips and the wicker creaked mildly beneath his weight, its dry interlacings stretched and shifting.

"Oh, well," Laura murmured, embarrassed, and looked out across the channel again. The breeze had come up, and boats were beginning to stir in the harbor. A Boston whaler chugged steadily through the moored sailboats, the shirt on the man at its stern brilliant white in the sunlight.

She could see that Ward thought they would get married, that they would settle in against each other, shrugging and pushing until the shape of each of them and the shape of the thing that held them was right, one offering a yielding curve where the other pushed a jutting bone, hard against soft, knob against hollow, the shape of it curved and complete. This frightened Laura, who believed that entropy governed the world, the universe and the dinner hour. She would have preferred his vision to her own, but could not believe in it. She feared the collision of the two; more, she feared the triumph of her own.

They took Sammy with them to the airport. On the way he and Ward played the alphabet game with the signs and Laura helped Sammy win.

"Where is Ward going?" Sammy asked.

"I forget," said Laura.

"California and Colorado," said Ward.

"California and Colorado," repeated Laura. The names sounded just right: rich, bright, exotic. Ward was a lawyer in the entertainment business, and his meetings seemed glamorous and arcane to Laura. She could not imagine the meticulous notings of fact, the conscientious regard for order, the deadening burden of precedent. These meetings, with charts and notes and references and opinions, all seemed risky to Laura. Things in general seemed to her so risky that it would be dangerous to move them around. She didn't want to learn more than she already knew.

"When will you be back?"

"Friday, by dinner, I hope. Maybe Saturday. I'll call."

Four days without him, thought Laura. In the mornings, while Sammy was at sailing class, she would work on her pictures in the darkroom she had rigged up. She had been thinking about a new series. She planned to work during the brightest part of the day, in the dim little dressing room hung with black curtains, watching the images, bringing them slow and shimmering up from the light.

At the airport they stopped the car near the terminal. Laura slid into the driver's seat, and they watched Ward walk toward the bleak concrete building, the sad institutional verge of grass rimming it. At the doorway Ward stopped and turned, pressing his fingers to his mouth, then throwing his hand into the air. He had always done this, saying goodbye to Laura. It always undid her: to make such a bold, public gesture, to take such a clear and simple stance. Surrounded by strangers, the air heavy with the jet-fuel kerosene stench, heavy mechanical winds swirling around him, weighted by the pressures of timetables, briefcases, professions, Ward turned fully toward her, without hurry, and sent her a whole and immaculate kiss.

When he had waved, he vanished into the revolving door, and, past that, Laura could not distinguish his silhouette from the other businessmen—raincoated, briefcased—who strode briskly toward the distance.

Laura took Sammy to the bumper cars on the way home, and then stopped for lunch. By the time they got back it was midafternoon. Richie and Sarah's car was not there.

When they opened the big oak front door, they stood still for a moment, listening. The house had been built in the 1890s, for the families of two brothers. It had two main doors, one on the front and one on the side of the house, and two staircases in the front hall, side by side. In between them was a sliding panel that could be drawn across to cut the hall in half. On each side of the house were a hall and a sitting room, and upstairs the two sides of the house mirrored each other. There was only one kitchen, and one set of stairs down to the lower floor. Laura wondered which family brought the cook or if they had alternated years? And did the families meet at mealtimes, as though they lived in separate houses, keeping the panel closed across the hall? Or was it drawn across in the midst of furious arguments, the brothers standing red-faced on the worn Oriental rug, the thundering of the sliding wood drowning out the violence of their words? Laura listened for a moment to the silent house, but there was no sound. At one end of the hall was a moose head, its blurry antlers holding caps from school teams. He stared straight ahead, his furry throat absurdly rising from the paneled oak.

Laura started upstairs with Sammy. The grown-ups had taken the large bedrooms on the second floor, that overlooked the water. On the third floor were the servants' rooms: odd-shaped, with slanted roofs, and the feathery branches of the treetops brushing against the windows. Pia and Karin and Sammy had these, and Laura rather envied them the rooms—they were faded and dreamy and cozy. Those three looked out over the water, though there were more rooms over the front—two more bedrooms that were empty, and the linen closet, and box-rooms.

Laura told Sammy to get his bathing suit and she would take him to the beach. She strode quickly along the second-floor hall, and flung open the door to her room. Sheba flashed under the bed. Upstairs there was a heavy footstep, a pause, and then another.

"Sammy?" she called, but his room was on the other side of the house. She went up to the third floor, calling again. The room over hers was Karin's, and the door was shut. "Karin?" she called, but there was no sound. She waited, then heard the heavy oak creak again. Laura turned around. "Sammy?"

Sammy was in his room, on the floor. He had found something mechanical that required careful attention. Laura hesitated in his doorway. She did not want to open the door and find a crazyman standing there, a gap between his teeth, a shotgun pointing casually at her feet. Nor did she want to open the door and have Karin hurl some wild adolescent bolt at her—what right did she have in opening up the door? She breathed silently, listening. She heard the creak again. Perhaps she should just pick Sammy up, holding her finger to her lips, and tiptoe down the stairs. By the time she came back from the beach, there would be no heavy creaks from the floor above her room, no sullen silence from Karin's closed door. Better the devil you do know, she thought.

She flung open Karin's door. Karin stood in the middle of the room, her face turned a patchwork of sullen rage.

"What is it? Can't you knock?" Karin asked.

"Can't you answer when someone says your name right outside your door? How did I know it was you in there?"

Karin sat heavily down on the bed. It was the kind without innersprings, and the whole thin mattress curved into a bow across the rusty springs supporting it. Karin stared at her feet.

"What happened? Where are the others?" asked Laura, her voice losing its sharpness. Karin seemed truly dejected. She did not answer. "How was the picnic?"

"Shitty," she said distinctly.

"What happened?" asked Laura again.

"Dad's such an asshole," said Karin. She leaned her elbows on her knees, her legs spread apart in the wrinkled skirt.

"Well?"

"Well." Karin looked up at her. "We took the picnic up Parkman Mountain, right?" Laura nodded. Karin checked her ankle, which seemed to need scratching. She attended to it. "He's such an asshole," she said, shaking her head. "They're both such assholes." Laura waited. "Well. We got to the top of Parkman Mountain. We got out the picnic basket. Everyone sits down on the grass. We have a clear view of the sound, and the water is this bright, clear dark blue, and you can see all the sails bellied out hard, as though they're solid because of the wind, it's really beautiful, and the sky is clear and the sun is out. Right?" Laura nodded, and Karin began to work on her ankle again. It was turning white where she was rubbing the grime off it. Laura wondered if Karin were tanned at all or merely dirty. "Well, we started unpacking everything, and I couldn't find my tofu anywhere. Which I happen to like, and which happens to be real food. So I asked everybody where it was." Karin paused. She stared out the window, as though she had momentarily lost track of the world. "Well, anyway, they were all eating this disgusting stuff. Ham and mayonnaise sandwiches. Blood and disease," she said, looking scornfully at Laura. "I knew I had put the tofu in. I mean, I knew it! What else would I have eaten, all that dead shit?"

Sammy was by now standing behind Laura, listening, and admiring the language. Irritated by this, Laura said, "What is the point, Karin? What actually happened?"

Karin stared at her, enraged. "The point is somebody came barging into my own bedroom without even knocking, that's the point, and I would like it very much if I could sit around in my own room for just one minute in peace."

Laura turned in one movement and picked up Sammy and swept him out. She shut the door and took Sammy downstairs with her, walking with swift, firm steps.

She took Sammy down to the beach, and sat among the pink-granite boulders and took pictures of Sammy's shadow among the rocks. The two things traded natures: the shadow, flattened and angled along the rough, sloping sides of the boulders, bore no relevance to human form at all, while the rocks, in close focus, looked rounded, organic, not-quite-recognizable views of living shapes. The sun lowered slowly behind the humpbacked hills, and the ocean stretched out and flattened in the sunset, turning lead-colored and quiet, the waves smoothing out and settling down, its colors losing brilliance with the light.

Three

When Laura returned, she went down to the kitchen, where Richie and Sarah were cleaning out the picnic basket.

"Karin came back awhile ago," she said. "I guess you knew."

"We did. Is she upstairs? Did she seem upset?" asked Sarah.

"A bit," said Laura.

"But I bet she didn't let on," said Richie. "Oh, that child doesn't give out a hint about what's on her mind."

Laura laughed, but Sarah shook her head and said, "Poor Karin, she makes things so hard for herself." As she spoke she was scrubbing at the basket, digging out the corners, sponging off all the old stickiness. Laura remembered her ironing on Saturday mornings, in the house in Maryland, her lips pursed, her hands pursuing errant wrinkles, moving across the pale cotton with heat and weight and determination, forcing a smooth, perfect surface into being. "I think I'll go up to her," Sarah said, finishing with the basket and turning it upside down to drain.

"Want some tea?" Laura asked. "I'm making some."

"Good, I'll make a fire," said Richie. "It's turning chilly."

She brought the mugs into the dining room, and they both sat down in front of the wood-burning stove.

"Now, tell," Laura said; "tell about the picnic."

"Didn't Karin?"

"Not specifically. I gathered it wasn't a great success."

Richie snorted. "That is correct. We climbed Parkman Mountain, and everyone was in a great mood, and there was a race going on and we watched that, and admired the view, and the sky and the wind and all, and then we sat down and spread out the picnic. And we all began to eat, except for Karin who couldn't find her tofu. Which she distinctly remembered putting in. She looked and looked. We all helped. Sarah looked and looked. No tofu. I began to eat my sandwich, which made her furious. There were other things she could have eaten, lots, and we all suggested that she eat them instead, but she only wanted tofu. Nothing else would do.

"Then she began to yell at us. She said somebody must have taken her tofu out of the basket. Someone who disapproved of her eating habits but was too cowardly to say so. And that we were all assholes. Then I told her that if I heard that word again I would wash her mouth out with soap."

Laura began to laugh. "Oh, dear."

"Then Pia got up to salvage the picnic, to keep Daddy and Karin from ruining the day. She said she would find the tofu. She started rummaging in the basket. We all watched, in suspense, hoping she could pull it off. It was like watching a magician. All of a sudden Pia said, 'Here it is!' She pulled it out of the cheese box and handed it to Karin. We all said good for you, and how clever, and well done. Pia beamed, and Karin unwrapped it and threw it in Pia's face and yelled, 'I suppose you think that's funny, you stupid birdhead!' Then Pia started to cry and I stood up and began to yell at Karin, and Pia threw it back at Karin and Sarah told them not to throw food and Karin screamed at the top of her lungs that she hated all of us and she took off down the mountain."

Laura let out her breath. "That's the worst," she said, shaking her head, "the worst. What was it that Pia thought was tofu?"

"Moldy cheese. It must have been in the refrigerator since the house was built."

Laura giggled. They were sitting on a small braided rug in the middle of the floor, in front of the stove, as though they were on an island. They sat companionably side by side, their elbows hooked over their knees, the steam rising from their mugs.

"I didn't know Sarah when she was that age, but I can't imagine that she was like Karin," said Richie.

"She wasn't," Laura said promptly. "Sarah was perfect. She was busy bringing me up. She taught me how to ski and how to skate and how to read and how to sew. She got straight A's and never fought with anyone."

"Not with your father?"

"No one fought with my father. Anyway, he and Sarah were good friends. They were always going off on bird-watching expeditions together, things like that."

"Just the two of them?"

"The boys weren't interested, I was too young, my mother couldn't walk far. It was Sarah and my father. They played the recorder together, too. Lots of things."

"What about you?"

"You knew me at Karin's age."

"I did?"

"At Granny's, the first summer we all met. I was a year older than Karin, I was sixteen."

"Were you there?" asked Richie.

Laura looked at him to see if he were joking. He was not. Laura remembered her stay at Inchfawn as the whole summer, though it could not have been; she'd had a job for most of it. Still, she remembered a whole summer shared with Richie before Sarah had arrived at the end of it.

When Sarah appeared, Richie had turned his attention, like a great warm beacon, to her, and Laura had felt his withdrawal from her world. She had understood, when Sarah arrived, that Richie belonged to another species altogether.

Richie watched Laura's face, and she now laughed.

"Was I there," she repeated.

"I take it you were there."

"I was there. I was madly in love with you, you nit."

"You were? Oh, yes, you were. But you were so young. You were wonderful to look at," said Richie, "but you were like a temptation in a fairy tale, you know, where Prince Alexis is put into a room and told not to touch anything, and on the table is an enormous cake covered with iced cherries, and iced cherries are his very favorite things in the whole world, and if he so much as puts his hand out to touch one of them the cake will explode with a terrible bang, and the witch will appear in the doorway, and the prince will sink to the dungeons below the waves with his poor parents, and the palace will remain in the witch's hands forever."

"I see," said Laura, smiling.

"It was too risky. You were like some young goat, a baby goat, all goofy and capering. I couldn't believe you had any idea of what you were doing."

"Maybe I did know," said Laura, smiling at the fire burning deep in the iron stove.

"You were a baby, an infant."

"I was a year older than Karin."

"Dear God," said Richie, reminded.

Laura looked at him, the glasses pushed forward on his nose, his hair falling across his forehead: it was a blunt, rounded profile, the red light from the open stove falling on his skin. For the first time she thought of him as separate from her sister, at his work, at night, alone, surrounded by the sleeping house, his women laid to rest. She wanted to ask him, Do you get along with my sister; are you happy? Tell me that you love her, that you find in her all that you have ever hoped for.

Sarah walked in and stood in the doorway. "Well, that's over with. Now, what about dinner?"

Laura got up slowly, stretching. "What did you say to Karin?"

"I told her that we loved her, and that no one was making fun of her, and that she might have been a little over-sensitive. And that we loved her."

Impressed, Laura asked, "And what did she say back?"

Sarah would not repeat what her daughter had said. "She's having a hard time getting along with grown-ups right now."

"She said we were all assholes," translated Richie.

Karin came down to dinner after she had been called three times, and sat sullenly without speaking during the meal. After dinner Laura took Sammy up to bed, and, when she came down, she found Karin miraculousy thawed. Everyone was sitting out on the porch in the summer dark. Below, the sleek yawls and sloops were moored, their sails bound and neat, their hulls swinging together, obedient to wind and tide.

They could see the lights, faint and shifty across the water from the boats with people on them. Laura sat in a rocking chair in the corner. They were playing Ghosts.

"It's you," Sarah said to her. "I've said 'F,' and that's as far as we've gotten."

" 'O,' " said Laura.

There was a silence, and Pia said " 'R.' "

It was Karin's turn, and there was a long pause while she tried to think of a letter that would continue a word but not end it. They could hear talking from the nearest boat in the channel below, a pretty yawl that had come in that morning, with wooden spars and a teak deck. It was big, about forty-five feet, and there were five or six people on board. There was laughter. They were very complete, that group, thought Laura, snug in their boat, food and friends gathered securely together in that wise, graceful craft. In the dimness of the porch, the tall dark pines leaning over them, the family all seemed separate from each other by comparison, strangers. Though from the boat, perhaps, they seemed complete, a unit.

"Wah! You're all against me," announced Karin, in an unbecoming imitation of a little girl. Pia made a disgusted noise in her throat. "I can't think of *any* letter that doesn't make a word, and I'm already 'GHO' and no one else is anything."

"You've been sitting in the fourth-letter place, babe," said Richie. "There are an awful lot of four-letter words. They start on me and end on you. Come over and sit next to me on the couch on the other side and we'll change the order." Karin got up and swished across the stone floor to her father, her long skirt swirling around her feet. Laura caught a faint, odd odor from her as she passed, and wondered if it were vegetarian, and if Karin smelled meat when she passed Laura.

Richie put his arm around her and pulled her into his lap. "You two should have come to the island with us last night instead of going to the dumb old movies," he said. "You can see movies anywhere. We had an ocean-going adventure."

Karin was not interested. "We saw a great movie."

"What was it?"

"It was this real old movie called *Casablanca.* Did you ever hear of it?"

The others laughed. Laura looked at Karin, interested. She was eight years younger than Ward. She was used to being teased for this, used to seeing herself as part of an arriving generation, still moist, unformed. Now she could see Pia and Karin thrusting blindly past her, relegating her to being older.

"That, my dove," said Richie, "is like my asking you if you have ever heard of E.T." He must have pinched her, Laura thought, because Karin squealed and giggled and complained, and the two of them wrestled in the dark.

"Let's go to England next summer," said Richie suddenly.

"I thought you were going to come here again," said Laura.

"We'll do both. I think we should rent a farm in the Cotswolds, and every morning we'll go out and bring in the fresh milk and cream and eggs and have tea and scones for breakfast. And then we'll go out bicycling along the lanes all day and stop later on and have hot scones for tea."

"We just had them for breakfast," complained Pia. "What are scones, anyhow?"

"I won't be able to go," said Karin importantly.

"And why is that, my dove?" asked Richie.

"I'll be living in a commune by then."

"You will not be living in a commune by then," said Richie, giving her a spank on the thigh.

"Anyway, communes are passé," said Laura bossily. "They're from the sixties."

"I'm from the sixties," Karin pointed out.

"Communes were started by people your age in the sixties. Don't you want to try something different?"

"I like communes," said Karin dreamily, suddenly losing her combativensss. "You could come with me, Dad, and Mom could too. But not the Blob."

"You make me throw up," said Pia, and Karin lapsed into high-pitched giggles, and Pia threw a pillow at her, which hit Richie, who grunted and said, "That's enough."

"Mommy, Karin's a pig and I hate her," said Pia. "Let's you and I go away together and eat steak." She moved her chair closer to Sarah's and leaned on her mother's arm.

"Murderer," said Karin. Sarah just laughed, and put her arm around Pia.

Laura was not used to being around adolescents. She had always thought of them, warily, as potential combatants, possible threats. But she could see that Karin and Pia were true companions and friends of their parents. Their lives were shared, they had woven themselves into something; they leaned against one another. She wondered, impressed, how Sarah had managed that; it was not what they had had as children.

Laura's childhood had been dangerous, filled with competition, suspicion, betrayals and rage. The youngest of four, Laura was inevitably the corpse, the victim, the body on whom the experiments were performed. Sarah, prim and teacherish, was her ally in private, but with the boys, in a group, Sarah might easily, coldly, heart-stoppingly turn against Laura, presenting a solid front of derision. For Laura, evading the hostility and contempt of her siblings had been a continual challenge. She lived in a dark, hazardous, children's world; the moments when she found herself in the region of her tall, good, distant parents were disorienting and unreal. *"Children, stop fighting,"* her father would say sternly, and the children, in the back of the car, would stop talking, confining themselves to fierce kicks and undercover punches. There seemed to be no connection between their world and the world of their parents.

But Sarah, Laura could see, had made something lovely, something strong and central, which would sustain the centrifugal demands of family life. She was glad to be seeing it; she was glad to be with them. They seemed so easy in their possession of this thing, it was like watching acrobats, leaning effortlessly into space, catching each other by the heels, trusting each other easily and absolutely, defying gravity, each leap an act of faith. Never having made it, Laura could not imagine making the leap, but it was before her; she could not deny its existence.

Four

When she was sixteen, Laura had gotten a job as a mother's helper with a family with five children on an inland lake in Maine. It was her first job away from home, and it lasted until mid-August. At the end of it she took a bus across the state to her grandmother's house in Bar Harbor.

Inchfawn was a summer house that had been built in 1892. It was shingle, with white trim, and two round towers at the ends, each with a round window. Big-windowed, high-ceilinged and large, it presumed an endless supply of servants and fuel. A deep porch ran along two sides of it, with a sloping, shingled roof, and broad steps led up to the front door from the circular driveway. Downstairs the rooms were large and pompous, and filled with dark, heavy oak, but upstairs furniture was simpler, white-painted wood and metal bedsteads, except in Granny's room, which held the beloved and funereal dark oak. The four big bedrooms on the second floor all had marble washstands with running water in them, but up on the third floor the bedrooms still had pitcher and ewer sets as they had when the house was built. Things had not been changed for decades. The curtains were worn to a wistful frailty, and if one were drawn up, away from the window, it would tear of its own fragile weight. Laura loved Inchfawn; she loved its size, its shabby elegance, its presumptions, its permanence.

She had never been to visit her grandmother alone, and had felt very grown-up, being there without the family. She had two weeks there before Sarah joined her; after Labor Day the two of them would go back down to Maryland together.

Granny was standing on the front porch when Laura arrived. It was deep, summer dusk, and Granny looked tiny, much smaller than Laura had remembered, an insubstantial figure among the shadowy chairs and big potted plants. But as soon as she spoke, she regained stature.

"Well, Laura."

"Hello, Granny," Laura said, and hugged her carefully. She seemed so fragile, Laura was afraid if she hugged her too hard she would hear a terrible snap. She was wearing a Paisley shawl wrapped around her shoulders, against the night air. She stood very straight.

"Come inside, this air is very damp," she said, and they stepped into the big, lofty hall, dark in the corners, the oak beams stretching up into blackness. Laura breathed in the old, faintly spicy, woody smell of Inchfawn.

"I'm so glad to be here," Laura said.

"Good," said Granny briskly, and turned away. "I've put you in the Garden Room," Granny went on. "You can take your things up and get ready for dinner. I'll see you in the breakfast room as soon as you're ready."

Laura took her things upstairs. The Garden Room was her favorite, looking out over the big back garden. Through the summer gloom she could still see the pale spires of hollyhocks along the fence. All the furniture was white, the big iron bedstead with brass knobs, the big dresser with the glass pulls, the spool-legged dressing table with a heavy gilt mirror over it. She unpacked, and brushed her hair, smiling at herself in the mirror, pleased to be alone in this house as Granny's guest. Going down the wide front stairs, she heard her footsteps clatter boldly through the house.

She said hello to Jane the cook, and found Granny in the breakfast room, a small, cozy room near the kitchen. "I take all my meals here now," Granny told her. "It makes no sense at all for Jane to traipse back and forth all the way to the dining room three times a day." But it was not Jane, still brisk and efficient, who was aging, Laura could see, it was Granny. Alone at the long polished table in the high-ceilinged dining room, Granny would have been lost, too old and too small, to command the room all by herself.

At dinner, Granny began her questions.

"Now, tell me, Laura, how was your job?"

"It was pretty good. It was fun. The people were nice."

"Are they friends of your parents?"

"I guess," said Laura, knowing what Granny meant. Granny was referring to the network of intrictate bloodlines and familiarity that stretched from Bar Harbor to Hobe Sound. Though Laura's father had deliberately removed himself from it, Granny spoke as though he still lived in that world, on East 88th Street in a town house, and as though Laura were going to Chapin, and the Gold and Silver Ball. Instead, Laura had grown up in the narrow farmhouse in Maryland and gone to the local flat, brick-faced public school. She had gone to a dancing school sponsored by the 4-H Club, held in a one-room schoolhouse, and run by the local postmaster. Laura was partly scornful of her grandmother's outmoded and crystalline snobbery, and partly wistful that she did not live in a town house and didn't at least have the option of rejecting the idea of a coming-out party.

"They live near us," said Laura, suggesting the possibility of a vague and purely geographically defined sort of friendship. She wondered if her grandmother minded that Laura's father had abandoned her serene and self-contained ship.

"But they were nice? And you enjoyed yourself?"

"Oh, yes," said Laura, depressed at her own tediousness. She did not know her grandmother well: what would interest her? What was it one said to grown-ups?

"The children were fun. I liked them," Laura said, and groaned inside. Other people, she knew, could carry on interesting conversations, could make their listeners laugh and sit up. Laura felt that perhaps she could do that, only she did not know how to begin. She did not know how to make things work.

Granny changed the subject. "Now, tell me, Laura, about your friends."

Of course she meant Boys. At her boarding school Laura saw Boys only at dances, every month or so. She had hardly ever talked to a Boy without washing her hair; without putting on those trickish, unnatural heels, raising her height and expectations; without shaving the soft feathery down from her legs, making herself smooth, clean, acceptable. Getting ready for the dances was more fun than the dances themselves: ironing dresses, putting on makeup and slithery new stockings. Running up and down the halls in bras and slips, in and out of each other's rooms, the girls complained exuberantly: the way the dress fit, the shape of one's legs, the way one's hair curled, the way one's hair wouldn't curl. Then came the sliding on of the silky, rustling dresses, the mealy, tasteless food at dinner, and at last the clattering down the long, dim hall, freshly waxed, unfamiliar with its darkened windows and empty classrooms, and finally the entrance into the vast, dangerous space of the gym.

Each time, Laura thought that this might be the night when she turned out to be just the person her partner wanted, who said just the right things, with the right cadences. But it had not yet happened: they were such difficult, alien creatures. She could not imagine being friends with one.

"My friends?" Laura shifted in her chair.

"Have you any beaux?" Granny asked.

"Sort of," Laura said: there was a boy from Andover who had written to her last year. But he was strange. "No one in particular," she admitted, and Granny nodded. "Did you have beaux, at my age?"

"Well, we did." Granny smiled at her, raising her eyebrows trimly, "but we weren't allowed to *call* them beaux until we came out." Granny had a habit of raising her chin at the end of a sentence and tightening her lips to finish the thing off, like a piece of sewing. She did this now, and rang for Jane to bring the dessert. Laura wondered what Granny did on the nights when she was alone, after dinner. She imagined her sitting bolt upright in her small, faded scarlet armchair in her bedroom, the lamp throwing a dense yellow light over her brilliant white hair. Maybe she had the radio on, as well: maybe there was a channel in Bar Harbor that had someone reading Dickens in the evening.

When dinner was over, Laura walked slowly with her grandmother to the broad front stairs. She kissed Granny good night and shut her eyes for a moment, her cheek against her grandmother's tissue-paper skin, smelling of Devon Violets. "Good night, Granny," Laura said, "I *love* being here. I love it."

Inside her own big, dim room, the light was on, and Laura could hear the moths fluttering and bumping against the screen. She closed the door and stood still. The house was soft and silent around her. She waited; she felt the presence of the house swirl and thicken like smoke. She was alone; she was quite alone. She took off her dress, dropping it gently in a pale heap on the braided rug. In her underwear, she sat at the dressing table and looked at herself in the mirror. She leaned forward, curious, the vast dim house behind her. She stared at her face, feeling as always, a vein of secret, voluptuous guilt.

When Laura was five, she had stood one day before the

full-length mirror in the room she shared with Sarah. Her own, known features were fascinating to her: there she was, a real presence. There were the outsides of her thoughts, her feelings, for the rest of the world to see. Eyes flashing, hands on hips, she was miming a confrontation in the middle of a royal saga. She was acting all the parts herself: queens, kings, princesses and the odd, craven maidservant. It was amazing to her—liberating—that she had this visible reality, like everyone else.

Slowly, she became aware of her father standing in the doorway, silent, unsmiling, grim. She stopped in mid-gesture, her hands still on her hips, her head half-tossed in queenly defiance. She met his eyes, her heart sinking, in the mirror. Her father stood for a second without speaking, his disapproval gathering force. In the silence, shame began to flood through Laura. But what was it she was doing? She waited, fearful.

"If you can't keep from looking at yourself in the mirror, we'll have to take it out of your room," her father said sternly. "Vain," he added, in case her crime was not clear.

Laura stayed motionless, her head still half-tossed, unwilling to acknowledge defeat, and for a moment they had stayed like that, her father's cold, critical stare meeting hers in the forbidden silver arena of the mirror, Laura's head lifted defiantly in a challenge that had not been meant for him but which it was too late to change. And this was the image that Laura held afterward: her father cold, censorious; herself vain, defiant.

Alone in her room at Inchfawn, Laura examined herself. Her eyebrows were thick and dark, with a mournful slant to them. In one of her marbled-blue eyes there was a sliver of hazel. Below the semicircles of confused lashes, there were wide pools of bluish shadows before the rise of the cheekbones. As always, Laura tilted her head slightly upward, so the pools caught the light, and disappeared. Her nose—long, narrow, with an ignoble upslant at the end—was dappled with faint russet specks. Her lips were chapped, tiny creases fanned out from its center. Her face was oval; the features were regular and so familiar that Laura had no idea what she looked like. One evening when she was twelve she had been alone in the upstairs bathroom, lolling dreamily in the tub. The windows were dense with steam, the pale-pink walls covered with a thin mist. Laura lay stretched full-length in the deep hot bath, her head against the wall, her hair drifting in the warm water. She pushed herself gently forward and back through the water, feeling the slow, deep surge of it against her legs, her back, her wrists. Enclosing her was the cloudy plastic shower curtain; through it she could barely see the old, painted linen cupboard, the wicker laundry hamper. Everything around her seemed barely real, floating, obscured. She felt peaceful, disembodied, without needs.

The door opened, and her mother came in. "Do you mind if I just slip in for a moment to brush my teeth?" Her mother smiled at Laura, who shook her head benevolently. Her mother, in her rose-colored cardigan, stood at the clouded mirror over the sink. The two of them shared the warm, pink, private world, the steamy air, the silence. Laura turned her head slowly back and forth, feeling her hair swish through the deep water.

"I'm going to let my hair grow," she told her mother.

Laura's mother shut off the water and turned to her.

"Good," she said. "Long hair suits you. You're beautiful, you know."

The word was like some dreadful, lurid lightning; in its too-vivid flash Laura saw herself set apart, willy-nilly, from other people who were not Beautiful. She knew the knowledge was illicit; her mother would never have said this in her father's presence. Later, alone in bed, she examined the idea—shocking—over and over.

Having this forbidden power had somehow frozen Laura. She felt this beauty was larger, more powerful than she was herself. It overwhelmed her.

Now, gazing at herself in the mirror at Inchfawn, Laura half closed her eyes and leaned back, wondering what the face looked like to other people. She moved her head slowly from side to side, feeling the dry, soft slither of her hair, on her naked back. Opening her eyes, she began to brush her hair, pulling the light, foamy mass of it away from her face, taut away from her temples, letting it fall back onto her shoulders. Behind her, in the mirror, the window was open to the night, framed by the faded curtains. She felt herself surrounded by the muted elegance of the house, the high ceilings, the dull brass of the old bedstead, the soft, worn sheets. Beyond her was the great unknown night and an unfamiliar wind. She was alone in this strange, new place. Filled with daring, she whispered aloud. *"I am beautiful,"* she said dangerously, and she wondered, breathing in the night air, what would happen.

In the morning the smooth cotton sheets were pale with sun. The view from the window was neat, domestic. The face Laura saw in the mirror as she brushed her hair was a child's. The boldness of the night before hovered around her still: she felt she had taken a great step.

Granny was already in the breakfast room when Laura went in. Granny sat up very straight, and her hair was in a tidy bun. Her hair was a thin, bright shimmer over her head. It was absolutely white, not blue or lavender, like most old ladies. Laura admired this.

"Good morning," said Granny. "Did you tell Jane what you'd like? Let me pour you some tea. Now, what are your plans for the day?"

"I have no plans for the day," said Laura, "but I'd like to

see your garden. I'd like to help you in it, if there's anything to do." Granny's gardens were famous: lush, sprawling, filled with bloom, her borders rose and fell against white-painted fences and tall, dark hedges.

Granny smiled, "There is always something to be done in a garden," she said. Her pearly skin was dry, pulled strictly across the bones of her skull. Her eyes were blue, pale, with uneven white rims around them. Laura could see nothing of herself in her grandmother, but she was glad she shared her blood.

After breakfast she took Laura out to look at the garden. All around the back lawn was a deep herbaceous border. A flagstone path down the center of the lawn ended in a round rose garden, edged with brick. After that was more lawn, and away at the end of it was a grape arbor; and underneath it were rustic wooden chairs on a flagged terrace. The air was heavy, and great insects droned as they drifted among the flowers. The smells rose slowly through the heat.

"It's a beautiful garden," said Laura. "Tell me about it." She knew nothing about plants.

Granny turned to her. "Tell you what about it?"

"Everything," said Laura simply. She wanted to possess something the way Granny did; she wanted to possess all the knowledge and the labor and the sights and smells of a garden. She wanted to look over it, as Granny did, with an air of calm dominion.

Granny moved forward. She wore a faded cotton dress with a self-belt that hung loosely at her waist. From behind, with her dark stockings and narrow hips, she looked like a young girl, if you ignored the flyaway white bun. Granny leaned over to a flower at the back of the bed, a tall spire of blue cup-shaped flowers.

"This is a bellflower," she said, "campanula." She pulled off a faded blossom. "You have to pull these off as they die or else they'll go to seed." She looked back at Laura, and added, "That means they'll stop blooming. They grow like weeds. I'm very fond of them, but I'm afraid Thomas thinks they're rather common." Thomas was Granny's gardener.

"Is he here today?" Laura asked.

"He only comes twice a week now," said Granny. "He's getting on. They're easy to grow, anyway." She stepped back from the bellflower, her espadrilles leaving a faint child's print in the black earth. "All you do is divide them. This is bee balm," she said, pulling at a rough, untidy mop of red. "Monarda. Smell," she said, and gave Laura a leaf and three narrow petals. Laura sniffed: it had an odd, aromatic tang. "It's also called horsemint, or Oswego tea. You can make tea from it, though I never have. The bees love it."

For an hour Granny named her flowers for Laura, explaining oddities and habits and history. "This is a new heather, George McDonald. I'm trying it out, in with these iris. It's an odd combination, but I think I like it."

Granny and I are an odd combination, thought Laura. I like it, too.

The garden had been a lucky choice: it interested them both. Laura liked it even more than she had expected, the shapes and colors intrigued her. She leaned closer to the plants. The leaves, the flowers, the stalks, all were different, but the shapes and angles echoed each other. She knelt. "I love the way they look," she announced. Down lower, they looked entirely different. She got closer. They created a world, light, airy, dense, green, immensely intricate. She stared into the interlacing green and remembered that her grandmother stood next to her.

"They're very complicated, aren't they?" asked Granny.

"Very," said Laura, unsure of what sort of complication her grandmother meant. She asked the name of a large yellow lily. She liked its regal demeanor, the waxy purity of its stance. It was perfect against the dark hedge, and the idea appeared in her head that she wanted to keep that image, simply to keep it. She would photograph it. The idea appeared full-blown, from nowhere. She had never taken a picture in her life.

Granny left her with a set of very careful instructions and a three-pronged fork. Laura weeded carefully, pulling up the long, resistant roots of the thistles, scrabbling for the rest with her fingernails when the root broke halfway. Leaning down closer to her prey, she began to examine the stalks and leaves. The closer she got to them, the better they looked. She lay down, finally, her head beneath a group of blue delphiniums. The pattern they made, the rhythms of the interlacing uprights and crossbars entranced her. The pale undersides of the leaves lay one against the other in receding progressions toward the deep blue of the sky, showing in small patches through the leaves. She stared up, moving her head from time to time, watching the patterns shift like the bits in a kaleidoscope. She could not draw, but she wanted to record that delicate geometry, somehow, to trap that intricate vision.

She had saved the money she had made that summer, and had nearly five hundred dollars waiting to be spent. The next day she had gone into Bar Harbor and found a camera shop. The man who ran it showed her Nikons, which had just come out. He told her they were the best in the world. Laura held one in her hand, but it was heavy and awkward. She couldn't fit her fingers around it easily; the distances, the construction of it were wrong for her. "I don't like it," she had told him, as though she were a great connoisseur of cameras, and handed it back. He had then given her a secondhand Leica, an M-2, to try. Laura picked it up. It fitted neatly into her hand, and her fingers knew exactly how it worked and what the weighting of it was. She looked through the viewfinder and was astonished at how greatly this act changed the process of looking. Even her hand on the counter, through the lens, took on a charged, magical significance, as though she now had a means to confer importance on chosen sights and objects.

She put the camera down. "This," she said to the man, and began pulling out her money.

The next day she had met Richie. He had been brought over by one of Granny's friends, a Mrs. Jameson: he was her nephew. They arrived in a 1938 Ford, which Mrs. Jameson's husband had driven up from Philadephia when he had bought it, in July of 1938. The car had never left Maine since, and it looked quite natural standing in front of Inchfawn. Granny had told Laura she was having someone to lunch, but Laura had not expected a young man. She was painfully shy and did not speak to him during lunch, answering Mrs. Jameson's questions carefully, then addressing herself to her plate. But after lunch the ladies had withdrawn to the porch, and Granny had firmly suggested that Laura show Richie the garden. Defeated, Laura dawdled down the back-porch steps in front of him. "That's the herbaceous border," she said, waving a vague hand at it.

"What is?" Richie asked, to make her look at him. She did; he smiled and she fell in love with him. She found his kindness remarkable. She had not known a young man with such kind eyes, such a gentle face, and he had smiled at her only to make her relax.

Bar Harbor did not then have a large summerhouse community, it was mostly day-trippers and people in motels. The summerhouse people had gone farther west along Mount Desert Island, after the Bar Harbor fire, to Northeast, Seal and Southwest harbors. She and Richie had a quiet time of it together. He had been working for an architect all summer and was now doing carpentry for his aunt until Labor Day. After work he came by for Laura, and they played tennis, or climbed mountains, or went down to the beach.

Laura hoped he would fall in love with her. She imagined that he had. One day they went up to the rounded top of a soft blue mountain. They stood bent over in the hot sun, searching out the small, dark, sweet blueberries, watching for snakes, scratching their arms and legs in the high bracken. It was a lonely mountain; they saw no one. When she had filled her basket, Laura lay back in the grass, among the tall ferns, her long, brown legs scratched in white patterns, like frost on a windowpane. Richie looked down at her against the grasses, the ground beneath her still hot from the day. She closed her eyes, pretending drowsiness.

"I can't walk," said Laura, shading her eyes and looking up. "I'm done in." She hoped he would lie down next to her; she hoped he would take her in his arms and do wonderful things to her, and that her life would be changed.

"Here, I'll help you," Richie said. He picked up her feet by the heels and began to drag her across the rough hillside.

At the end of the summer, Sarah arrived at Inchfawn. She had been at school, studying kinship patterns in Indonesia. The day she arrived, Laura and Richie were playing tennis, and when they returned, Sarah was upstairs unpacking. Laura, with Richie behind her, had gone in to find her. She stood at the foot of the stairs and called out, "Sarah?" She had one foot on the bottom step and one hand on the bannister. Sarah came out onto the landing at the top of the stairs, smiling. She was wearing a neat round-collared white blouse and plaid Bermuda shorts, long, unwrinkled. Her hair was a shining short cap. "Hello," she said, poised, relaxed.

As soon as she saw her, Laura, teetering on the bottom step, asymmetrical, off-balance, was conscious of her own sweaty face, her flyaway hair. She was wearing white cut-offs, not proper tennis shorts, and the ragged leg rims were fraying. Her sneakers were grubby. Shy, she did not bolt up the stairs to her sister: she saw her as Richie must—neat, demure, right.

"Come down and meet Richie," Laura said awkwardly, as though her sister were someone she hardly knew.

"Hello," he said. "Come down."

There was only a week left of the summer. The thin, clear air began to turn sharp and chill in the mornings. Laura watched Richie and Sarah form something in which she had no part. It began to darken during daylight hours. The summer was being taken from them, bit by bit.

Granny found Laura mourning in the garden. She said simply, "You're too young for him."

Laura yanked at a thistle root. "Oh, too young," she said. "What does that have to do with anything?"

"A great deal," said Granny firmly. "Also, you are entirely unsuited."

Laura tugged at the weeds and did not answer.

At Thanksgiving, at Christmas, when Sarah came home from college, she told Laura that Richie said hello. In the spring he came and spent a weekend in Maryland, and they announced their engagement. Laura saw all this as she would have watched the movements of great, vast, powerful clouds in the air high above her, out of her realm.

Five

During the week that Ward was gone, Laura began a new series of photographs: trees. She liked the contrasts, the filigree of the branches, the solid line of the trunk. She got up early and went out to the pinewoods at dawn to get the first light slipping through the rough trunks, the mist curling slowly up from the ground. When regular daylight took over, she left and went back home to take Sammy to his sailing classes. She worked in the darkroom until lunch, and began pinning the first prints up in the bedroom: she envisioned a wall of trees.

Sheba seemed to have reformed. She still shot under the bed when the door opened, but the rugs were pristine. Laura wondered if this meant that she would stumble on a horrid cache somewhere, for she never saw Sheba downstairs, and the Kitty Litter seemed untouched.

Ward called on Tuesday afternoon. Laura was in the village, and he talked only to Sammy. On Wednesday he called again, and Laura told him about the trees.

"Why trees?" he asked.

"You'll see," she said; "they're good. You'll like them."

"Good," said Ward, meaning it, and Laura smiled.

"How's your stuff going?" she asked.

"Okay," said Ward. "I'm meeting with the Lunatic today. He wanted to do an animal porn movie, I think."

"Good," said Laura; "nice for the children. No more violence."

"Yeah. Is Sammy there?"

"At the beach."

"Give him a hug."

"I will. When are you coming back?"

"I don't know. Friday or Saturday. I may have to spend a while on this."

"See you then."

"I love you," Ward said.

"I love you." Laura always waited for Ward to say this first. He always did; she was grateful.

On Thursday Laura was in her bedroom adding another print to her wall of trees. The wall was beginning to take on a mystical, delicate presence; the subtle insistence of the shapes and the fall of light were starting to become something. She considered her work, sitting on the bed and squinting her eyes. Pia called her to the telephone. She went out onto the landing and picked it up.

"Hi," she said cozily to Ward.

"Hi, Laura," said Nathaniel, her husband.

"Oh, hi," she said, backpedaling wildly.

"What's the matter?" asked Nat.

"Nothing," said Laura, "nothing. How are you?" The tone of her voice suggested that Nat was an old friend, someone to whom she owed the duty of friendship rather more than she felt the pull of it, but someone to whom the debt was scrupulously paid. This careful friendship was the prevailing mood between the two of them, but it was interrupted regularly by the violent eruption of their darker sides: the blame they leveled at each other and themselves for the dissolution of their marriage, the rage they felt at having failed, the swirls of bitterness, bitterness. Their separation papers had finally been signed and filed; they waited only for the court to pronounce them absolutely dissolved from one another.

"I'm fine, just fine," said Nat politely. "How's Sammy?"

"Terrific," Laura said energetically. "He's having a great time. He's at the beach right now. He's getting into some heavy sand."

Nat laughed. "A lot of, like, sand castles?"

"Really," Laura said, and they both laughed.

"I wish I could see him," Nat said, his voice was deliberately wistful. This intrusion of Nat's sprawling, demanding emotion was one reason Laura had left him. Another was his secretary, another was a stewardess he met on a midnight flight from Atlanta—there had been lots of reasons.

"You should see him," Laura went on, determined to ignore the pathos. "He's as brown as a sand crab. He's taking sailing lessons," she continued, babbling. "Sort of sailing lessons. What he does is climb into a dinghy and the counselors row them around, and they all sing songs and eat peanuts."

"Very nautical," said Nat. There was a pause. "They row him around, though? Out in the harbor?"

"In the cove, actually."

"But I mean, is that a good idea? I mean, Sammy's not the greatest swimmer in the world. I mean, is it really safe to have him rowing around in deep water? I mean, I'm sure you've thought of all this, but it really doesn't sound very safe to me. I really would urge you to think about this."

Laura said nothing for a minute. Nat seemed to think he was the only person in the world capable of linear thought.

"Gosh, I never thought of that," she said. "They wanted him to wear a life jacket, but I told them not to bother."

A wary pause.

"Oh, he does wear one, then," Nat said finally.

Laura did not answer.

"Well, that sounds great, then. Just great." His voice returned to hearty.

"He loves it," Laura said shortly.

"Good, good," said Nat. "How are the photographs coming along?" While he was married to Laura he had treated her photography with friendly contempt, as though she did flower arranging. Now he took it more seriously, not because he thought it more serious, but because he was afraid she would hang up on him. He talked about it as though it were a serious hobby, like breeding Weimaraners.

"Fine," said Laura.

"You sound kind of funny," said Nat. "Are you okay?"

"I'm fine," said Laura. She wished she did not get so easily angry at him. "How are you, anyway?"

"Well, I'm okay," said Nat, his voice denying it.

"What's the matter?" asked Laura.

It had been she who had left. Nat had begged her not to. "I'll change," he had promised. "Just tell me how you want me to be." But the fact that he had asked meant that Laura could not answer him. What she wanted was a man who drew his own outlines. She could not support them both, and while Nat was brainy, he had no common sense at all. It depressed her to know that she could never ask his advice. And she found that she could forgive him his tantrums, his women, but only from a great distance. At the end, she found herself light years away from him. When she finally told him she was leaving, she was already alone.

She had not wanted to hurt him. She felt she would have done anything for him except that one thing, staying on.

"Well, I've been thinking about Sammy," Nat said slowly. He was going to ask her for something. "With you up there all summer, I won't get to see him until after Labor Day," he went on.

"You could have taken him all of August if you'd wanted."

"I know, but the house didn't work out, and I couldn't find a babysitter—nothing worked out, so I'm not going to take any real time off."

There was a pause. "Well?" said Laura.

"I was wondering if it would be all right with you if I came up to see him."

How could she refuse to let Nat see his own son?

"I should think that would be fine," said Laura reasonably. "He'd love to see you."

"That would be great," said Nat heartily. "That would be really great. Would this weekend be okay?"

"Sammy has no plans," said Laura.

"Great," said Nat again. "I'll be alone. I wondered where I could stay."

Laura still loved Nat, in a way. She remembered loving him, she remembered his sweetness: she knew his sweetness.

"Well, you could stay here, I should think," she said slowly. She was not sure about this. "We have a lot of room." She did not see how she could make Nat stay in a motel, with four empty bedrooms in the house.

"Gosh, that would be terrific," said Nat, at last sounding genuine. "That would be just great. I really wasn't looking forward to staying in some dreary motel."

"No!" Laura laughed, relieved that she could offer Nat something he truly wanted. "No sense in that."

"That's awfully nice of you," said Nat. "I'll book a plane, then. What's the schedule like?"

"The Friday plane is full by now, I'm sure," said Laura. she wondered what it would be like in the evening, after Sammy went to bed, with Nat there. "I'd try the Saturday morning plane to Bangor."

"Well, I was actually thinking of coming on Friday," said Nat, "I could leave early." Laura did not answer. "I had actually sort of planned it." Laura said nothing, angry at his wheedling. "But maybe Saturday would be better for you," finished Nat.

"It would, actually," said Laura. "We're having some people here for dinner." Now she had lied to him.

"Oh, gee," said Nat, audibly polite, "I don't want to upset your plans." The Good Guest, thought Laura. "I'll be on the Saturday plane, then, unless you hear from me. How do I get from Bangor to Northeast Harbor?"

"Taxi," said Laura firmly.

When she hung up, she began to wonder if Nat's visit was such a good idea. Nat's seeing Sammy was undeniably a good idea, but all the trappings began to seem less good, and the more she thought about it the less good an idea the whole thing seemed. She imagined telling Ward. She had rather skimmed over the idea of Ward altogether while she had been talking to Nat. Now she admitted to herself: it was Ward who was paying for the house, and Nat would be his guest. The chances were slim that Ward would approve of her still-husband coming up for a visit under his roof. Well, she argued, it would only be for one night, and Sammy would be thrilled. She would explain it to Ward when he called.

But Ward did not call on Thursday. Laura expected him to arrive on Friday. In the morning she went out with her camera: it was a spectacular day, the sky was full of rushing clouds and flashes of white-hot sun. Ward had still not arrived by suppertime, and afterward they took the girls to see *Key Largo*. Laura thought Ward would be home when they got back, but instead there was a note by the telephone from Winifred, which Karin read out loud. "Laura: Ward called and said to tell you he'd be home tomorrow on the morning flight to Bangor."

"Tomorrow!" said Laura.

"Tomorrow," said Karin, looking at her. "What's the matter?" Laura did not answer. "Don't get mad at *me*."

"Laura's not mad at you, ducks. She's disappointed that Ward won't be back until tomorrow," said Richie.

"Darling Ward," said Pia, putting her hand to her heart. "How can we live without him?"

"Now Pia," said Sarah, smiling at her. "Who would like some Sleepytime tea?" With the smooth wings of hair on either side of her face, and the teakettle in her hand, she looked like an illustration for The Good Wife. Sarah was Order, thought Laura gloomily; she herself was Chaos.

"Nat's coming on the same plane," she announced.

"Nat?" everyone asked. Laura nodded, dazzled by her horrible revelation. Everyone stared at her.

"Why is Nat coming?" asked Sarah, getting out mugs.

"Oh, otherwise he won't see Sammy until Labor Day. He was going to take him in August, but then he didn't get the house he wanted, or something, so he didn't have anywhere to take him. He misses him," she finished, reminding them of larger issues than domestic arangements.

"Does Ward know he's coming?" asked Richie.

Laura shook her head. "I haven't talked to him—he hasn't called since I talked to Nat."

"What difference does it make to Ward if Nat comes?" asked Karin boldly. "Why is that such a big deal?"

There was a pause. "Well," said Sarah, slipping mugs neatly in front of everyone, "people who have been in love and then aren't have an awkward time of it. There's no framework of behavior for them."

"Maybe I should go and meet Ward and drive him back alone so we can talk," Laura said.

"And leave Nat to come back in a taxi?" asked Richie.

"I guess not," said Laura. They sipped at the tea, the hot

steam curling up from the mugs. Laura was appalled at what she had allowed to happen. How could she have done it? Ward would think she hadn't even thought it would matter. Imagine inviting her husband up to stay in Ward's house. She was crazy.

"I'm going to call Nat and tell him he can't come after all," she said. "I'll tell him something's happened."

"Laura, it's eleven-thirty," said Sarah.

"I don't care," said Laura. She was frantic.

She dialed Nat's number on the kitchen phone, and everyone watched her in silence. The phone rang and rang. She banged the phone down. "He's out carousing," she said accusingly, as though he should not have been.

"Then there's nothing for it," said Sarah; "we'll just have to make the best of it." She stirred her tea.

They sat and contemplated making the best of it. Laura contemplated the worst of it. Pia stared, fascinated, at the furious anxiety that radiated from Laura.

"Suppose I drive in, too, and pick up Nat," said Richie. "You can say you and Ward have to stop off somewhere on the way home."

Laura looked at him. Richie hated driving, and Bangor was an hour each way.

"If you don't do it that way," said Sarah, "either you'll have to pick them both up or they'll end up sharing a taxi."

The idea of Ward and Nat sitting in silence for an hour across the barren landscape was more than Laura could take.

"What about Sammy?" she asked.

"You take him in, and he can come back with me and Nat," said Richie. He was standing up, leaning over the table, supporting himself with one fist set beside his mug. His glasses glinted, turning his eyes unseen. His eyebrows were raised, waiting. The kindness of the gesture overtook Laura. Richie owed her nothing; she was not his sister or his wife. It was not even courteous; it was purely kind. Laura knew no response to this; she felt the unexpected swelling beneath her eyelids, and turned away.

"That would be very nice of you, Richie," she said, concentrating on her tea. "That would be very nice."

Six

The plane was late. Richie and Laura stood about, then went into the coffee shop. They each ordered tea, though Laura only sipped at hers; there was a gap where her stomach should have been. Richie went off to ask about the plane when it was twenty-five minutes late. Sammy had brought some trucks and was playing with them outside the window of the coffee shop. Laura watched him, his head down, moving the trucks slowly through the sand in front of him. His mouth was moving, but she could hear nothing.

Richie came back. "They don't know when it's coming," he said. "Boston's fogged in, and they don't even know when it will take off."

"It hasn't even left Boston?"

Richie shook his head. They stared at each other. The trip home was too long to make any sense. They were stuck there for at least an hour, even if the plane took off that instant.

"You go back," said Laura. "There's no point in ruining your day."

Richie shook his head again and smiled. "In for a penny, in for a pound," he said, sitting down. "We may as well have some more tea. We may as well order a whole samovar." They waited for the waitress in silence, watching Sammy outside the window.

"Or would *you* rather go back, and I'll take both of them?" asked Richie suddenly.

"Oh, no," said Laura, her eyes widening. "If I'm not here to apologize when Ward steps off that plane, I may as well start packing." As she said it Laura imagined the terror of being cast out, standing at the door of Ward's apartment, her bags around her. It would be more than suitcases now; she had settled in there. There were things that wouldn't fit in suitcases—books, lamps, pillows, plates. And whose were they all, anyway? Ward had been giving her household money for months—what was she, after all? Paid housekeeper? Mistress? Who was she? What was she doing? The image of herself at the doorway, surrounded by the litter of her belongings, was awful. *I must change,* thought Laura urgently, as though it were something she could perform on command, like washing her hair. *How should I be?*

"How long have you and Ward been together?" Richie asked, his eyes on Sammy. "Three years?"

"Only two," said Laura. "Well, two and a bit." When she had left Nat, she had done nothing about divorce. It had been Ward who had told her finally that she must. She had still been wearing her wedding ring. "Either you've left him or you haven't," Ward had said, but she had not answered.

"I don't think I've seen Nat since Sam was born," Richie said.

"It's very nice of you to do this," said Laura.

"I like Nat," Richie said. There was a long silence, and then he said gently, "I never knew why you two split up. You both seemed so glittery, to me; you seemed to have so much fun."

Laura never talked to anyone about leaving Nat. It would

have been easy to make it sound all his fault but she was hardly blameless. She had known what he was like when she had married him; what right had she had to cast him off?

She turned her head away. "Well," she said carefully, "we weren't really very committed to each other."

"What does that mean?" Richie asked. "How did you know you weren't really committed?"

The question made Laura uneasy: it was Richie's marriage she admired. "Well, you just know it. It's like knowing whether or not you're in love. And I wasn't in love with Nat. At least, I *loved* him, but I wasn't *in love* with him."

"Are you with Ward?" Richie asked. He watched Sam.

Laura shifted in the chair, molded plastic that did not match her own mold. "What do you think?" she asked, smiling.

He looked at her and did not smile back, but his eyes were gentle and friendly.

"That's not an answer," he said.

Laura looked at him for a moment. Ward and Nat, tense and unfriendly, were on their way toward her. She did not want the next twenty-four hours.

"Let's run away," she said, putting her face in her hands. "I don't want to go through all this."

"But do you? Love Ward?"

Laura could not answer. She had told Nat that she had loved him; she had told herself that she had loved Nat, but she had not. She no longer believed in her own instincts.

"I don't know," she said, aware that she was betraying Ward: he would not have answered that way. Richie turned back to the window. Laura wanted to ask if he loved Sarah, but did not dare.

She wanted to stop talking about herself and Ward.

"That summer we met I was in love with you, I thought," said Laura as if this should show Richie how unreliable her emotions were.

Richie smiled at her, and with a shock, Laura realized he felt sorry for her. She felt tears rise. Sammy appeared and stood before the table.

"I want something," he said.

"What would you like, Sambo?" asked Laura. She pulled him to her, soft boy-flesh, and breathed in the sandy brown smell of his hair.

"Something," he said expectantly.

Laura laughed, released. "Me too," she said.

As a treat, she ordered him an ice cream, and Richie checked again on the plane and was told it had taken off from Boston. Laura went to the ladies' room.

The ladies' room was large and tiled in beige. It stank of disinfectant, and there were rumpled paper towels all over the floor, right next to the empty wastebasket. Laura washed her hands slowly and looked at herself in the mirror. Her eyes were calm. She looked as though she had no thoughts. Why have you done this? she asked the face.

She went back out to find Richie and Sammy, and poured herself some more tea. It was cheap tea, thin and bitter. Sammy chatted cheerfully to Richie.

"Knock, knock," said Sammy.

"Who's there?" asked Richie. The loudspeaker announced something, but the voice was blurred.

"Banana," said Sammy, grinning. "Knock, knock."

A plane arrived, and people were moving toward a gate.

"Who's there?" asked Richie again.

"Banana," said Sammy. "Knock, knock."

Laura shifted so that she could see arriving passengers.

"Who's there?" asked Richie.

She wondered if they had sat next to each other on the plane, out of politeness. What would they have talked about?

"Orange," said Sammy,

"Orange who?" asked Richie.

People began milling toward them, a casual group with canvas carryall bags full of odd things, one or two men in business suits, the rest a summer crowd with open collars.

"Orange you glad I didn't say banana?" asked Sammy triumphantly.

"There's your father," said Laura, her heart contracting.

Nat's tense face appeared in the archway. He looked quickly around, saw Laura and Sammy and smiled as though they loved him. They all got up from the table, and Laura could feel herself smiling back as though he were her social inferior. Behind him she saw Ward, stony-faced, and tried to change her face to welcoming for him.

Laura took Sammy's hand and began to walk toward the two men. She squeezed him tightly, as though conceivably he were not paying attention, and said again, "Look, there's *Daddy.*" She was hoping that somehow Sammy's presence would blur the moment of arrival. Nat stopped, leaning over, and slapped his knees and called, as though to beckon a dog, "Sambo!"

Sammy had caught his mother's nerves, and stood frozen next to her. He did not admit to knowing Nat. Ward strode toward them. Nat blew Sammy a kiss. This was more than Sammy could take, and he suddenly put his arms around Laura's leg and flattened his face against her thigh, blocking out the view of his two worlds in collision.

Ward reached them and stopped. "Hi," he said, his voice light and unfriendly.

"Hello," said Laura. She lifted up her face to be kissed. It was not. Ward looked at Richie. "Hello," he said.

"Richie's going to take Nat and Sammy home," Laura said. "I'm going to take you."

Ward put his hand, very lightly, on Sam's head.

"Hi, Sam," he said, quietly, and then, since Sam did not move, he said, "See you later." He turned to Laura. "I'll go get my bag." Laura felt Sam's head swivel against her to watch him.

Nat came up smiling. "Hi," he said loudly, feigning ease. He kissed Laura on her cheek before she knew it; she jerked back, her flesh invaded. She looked back to see if Ward had seen, but he was gone.

"How are you?" Nat asked, as though she were a college classmate not seen in years, never well known. Nat crossed his arms on his chest and stepped closer to her, his voice confidential.

"Gee, you know, I hope I haven't upset things for you," he said.

Laura looked blank. "What do you mean?"

Nat blinked slowly. "I'm sorry Ward is so upset. I really thought—I mean, I imagined you would have told him I was coming up. He didn't seem to know anything about it."

"Don't worry about it," Laura said coolly.

"I'm really sorry," Nat said, drawling, nasal. He's reveling in all this, she thought.

"Don't be silly," Laura said. "Ward's not mad at all. I don't know what you're talking about. Here, Sambo, you go with Daddy and Richie, and I'll see you back at the house." Sam did not move. Laura jiggled at his arm. He did not move, his body was rigid along her leg. She could feel Ward waiting dangerously for her.

"Sammy," she said, patting his shoulder. He jerked away from her hand, burrowing his head deeper into her legs.

"Sammy?" said Nat sentimentally. "Little boy?"

They all waited.

Nat crouched down next to Sam. "Sam," he said, "I brought you something."

Sam whipped his face away from Nat to the other side of Laura's leg. "Where's Ward?" he demanded.

"He's in the car," said Laura. "He's waiting for me. You

go with Richie and Daddy, and Ward and I will meet you at home. Your Daddy is very glad to see you, Sambo, and I bet he doesn't know any of your Knock Knock jokes."

"I'm going with Ward," Sammy said in a hard, high voice.

"Don't you want to ride with me, Sammy?" asked Nat. Sam stayed rigid, his face turned away.

"I think we shouldn't force it," Laura said. "Don't make him think he's forced to be with you."

"Look," said Nat, "I didn't fly all the way up to this godforsaken place—"

"You asked if you could come here," Laura snapped.

"I didn't come up here so you and your—Ward could spend the weekend with my son. I want him to ride back in the car with me."

"I'm not trying to *keep* you from riding in the car with your son," she said. "Of course you can force him to go with you."

"He'd be perfectly ready to come with me if it weren't for the way you're acting," said Nat.

"Me?" said Laura. "What am I doing?"

"I can see what you're doing," said Nat. "You can make Sam feel any way you want him to."

"I am not trying to make Sam choose between us," Laura said. "It is utterly unfair to accuse me of that. As a matter of fact, you will never have any idea of how hard I try to let him know he doesn't have to choose. I try very hard to make sure he looks forward to seeing you. I make sure he knows he should love you, no matter how much of an asshole you are."

"Uh," said Richie, looking at other things.

Nat turned to him and shrugged his shoulders. Laura was now furious with herself: she could never quite keep her self-control long enough, with Nat.

"Why don't you and I take off?" Richie suggested to Nat.

"Women and children first," he said, smiling at Laura and giving her a sweeping bow. Nat turned on his heel as though he had been dismissed, and began walking toward the baggage claim. Richie gave Laura a little salute, and then she and Sammy started out for the parking lot, and Ward. Sammy hung on to her leg like an anchor.

Seven

In the car Laura tried to get Sammy to sit on her lap for protection, but he refused and climbed into the back seat, where he sat staring out the rear window. No one spoke. They drove through the empty airport land, useless grassland with flat-roofed buildings made of corrugated tin. On the other side of Bangor was Ellsworth, a sad section of sagging Victorian houses with peeling paint. Past the dying houses was a neon strip: fast-food cupolas, lawn furniture, used-car dealers with strings of flapping flags across the sky—all those moveable, interchangeable shops and setups that always seem desolate, no matter how bright their colors or how bold their displays.

"Well," she said, feeling the silence pile up against her, "I'm sorry."

"Sorry for what?" asked Ward.

"Everything. I'm sorry I didn't talk it over with you—"

"Did you try?"

"I didn't know where you were."

"My office did."

"I thought you'd call me."

"I did."

"I thought you'd be back on Friday; that's what I was expecting."

"I never said definitely I'd be back on Friday. I said specifically I might be back on Saturday. Didn't it occur to you that I might, in fact, get back on Saturday, as I said I might?"

"I just didn't think. I mean it didn't hit me until I got home on Friday night and found you not there. And then I couldn't call your office."

"I thought you might have told Winifred to ask for my number if I called. Or you might have left her a message: 'Tell Ward I've asked my husband up for the weekend.' "

Ward had not looked at Laura once. She said nothing. They drove on without speaking until Ward said, still without turning toward her, "What's your plan, Laura?"

"Well," said Laura carefully, "we won't be spending that much time together. I mean, Nat can take Sam for a walk this afternoon, and he'll—

"No," said Ward. "I mean, what is *your* plan?"

"My plan?" repeated Laura.

"Do you think you'll just go on living in my apartment month-to-month like a tenant without a lease?"

They were driving up a long, gradual hill. Beside the road there were squat little modern bungalows. Everything about them was mean: the asbestos shingles, the wavy-edged fake clapboards, the shutters with moon and heart shapes cut in them. They were all disorderly, old tires lying in the yards, straggly plants along the roadside, tilted television antennas. One of the houses had a sign outside of it: ELMER'S JUNQUE. The whole yard was filled with litter, rusty scraps from other people's households, strange complicated machinery, two washing machines, a refrigerator hulk on the porch. Just past the scraggly yard were the pine trees. All the hills around were covered in a thick, luxuriant green, stretching up to the crest of the hill they were on, and the hill after that, and the one after that; the green pinewoods went on and on, unimaginably. The tall, straight trees made the cramped little houses look worse than they were, crouched along the road like beggars.

Hearing Ward's question, Laura stared out of the window and began to hate the view; she hated in particular the people who lived in those damp, hopeless houses surrounded by trash, people who lived in the shadow of a natural propriety and ignored it, people who could not simply take hold of their lives and order them and live decently and properly. Laura hated the people. She closed her eyes; she did not answer.

"Well?" he said. Laura opened her eyes. They had reached the top of the hill, and the forest spread out around them, rolling in long swells to the skyline. There was no end to it.

"What's *your* plan?" she asked. She swallowed.

"I want to marry you," he said, making it sound like a threat. "But it's not only my decision."

Laura did not speak. She turned her head away from Ward. The thought of it gave her a rising panic, as though she were running out of air.

They drove the rest the way home in silence. Sam had gone to sleep in the back seat. When they got home, Nat was already there, standing on the lawn, his arms crossed on his chest, his legs apart like a hollow-chested giant in a children's book.

Ward said, "It can't go on like this forever." He got out of the car without looking at Laura, and walked past Nat, nodding to him as he passed.

Laura got into the back seat with Sammy. She took him in her arms and began to rock him back and forth. Sam just exactly fit her embrace, his warm solid limbs the perfect size for her arms. His eyelids still, shut, he made faint smacking noises with his mouth. Beneath the translucent lids, she could see his eyes moving, watching secret things. She wanted to see everything Sammy saw; she wanted him still to be a part of her body. A faint rim of white lay ragged around one corner of his mouth: in her own mouth Laura could taste the thick warmth of sleep. She kissed Sammy hard, on the cheek, and he opened his eyes.

"Hi," she said, but he did not answer. She pulled him backward out of the car, and carried him out to Nat, staggering under his unhelpful weight.

"I'm sorry I got so angry," Laura said civilly to Nathaniel. Sammy had heard the fight, he ought to hear a polite resolution.

But Nat did not want one. "I would have thought," he said stiffly, "that you could have restrained yourself in view of"—he nodded at Sammy—"the audience. But I should have known that you couldn't."

"I said I was sorry," repeated Laura, furious again.

"Okay, okay," said Nat magnanimously. "We'll forget the whole thing." He leaned over Sam. "Hi, kid."

Sam stared at him.

"Hi, Sam." Nat put his face next to his son's.

"Hi, Daddy," Sammy said, his face suddenly shifting from sullen, private sleep to radiant sociability. "Come and look at my new truck. I have a new truck."

"You do?" asked Nat, delighted.

"Come on," said Laura, as though they were friends. "Let's go show Daddy your truck, and your room, and his room, and everything." They walked across the lawn together, the three of them, like a family. As she opened the front door Laura suddenly imagined the sliding panel would have been pulled across, that she would stand with Nathaniel in their side of the house, banned from everyone else. But of course it was not; the empty stretch of floor lay undivided end to end, the moose head still presiding absurdly on the far wall, the harbor glimmering through the windows.

Laura took Sam and Nat up to their rooms on the fourth floor. She left them together and went back downstairs, sniffing uneasily along the halls. She did not trust Sheba.

She found Ward in their room, sitting on the bed, his briefcase open before him, papers all over the spread. Sheba was lying next to him, her tail neatly covering her nose. She opened one gold eye as Laura came in.

"Hi," said Laura desperately.

"Hello," said Ward, writing. He did not look up.

There was a pause.

"Look," said Laura, but she could think of nothing to follow. "Do you want to play some tennis?"

Ward raised his head and stared at her. "No," he said, "I do not want to play some tennis." He went back to his papers. Laura stood in the doorway, but he did not look at her again.

"I really am sorry, Ward," she said. "I'm *terribly* sorry."

"You can't undo things by apologizing."

"You can't hold things against people forever."

"I'm not," said Ward. "I'm waiting for an answer to my question."

Laura wondered why she had come into the room. She had nothing to say. She waited until he went back to his yellow legal pad again and then she left.

She went back up to the fourth floor, remembering that she had not made up Nat's bed. She felt as though she might fly out of her skin, as though the molecules that composed her body and all the minute operations within it had turned to particles of glass, that every movement taking place inside her body—the narrowing of the capillaries, filling of the bronchi—was producing an unbearable glittering scrape.

The linen closet was on the fourth floor. It was large, almost the size of a dressing room. It had white birch shelves from floor to ceiling, piled with soft, old white linens. The first time Laura had gone in there she had stood for a moment, the door half-shut behind her, and pressed her face against the smooth, white sheets, smelling the faint cinnamon smell of unfinished birch.

Today the door was ajar when she reached it. As she opened it she realized she had found Sheba's horrid cache. The room stank. The soft white sheets were rucked and stained, piles of black mess lay on everything, dribbling dark stains touched each layer of the piles. The shelves themselves were blackened—deep, dark-brown rings seeping into the pale wood. The smell was foul.

Laura closed the door behind her and stalked downstairs to their bedroom, stiff with fury. She opened the door. Sheba caught her eye and was under the bed in a flash. Laura shut the door behind her and turned the knob until she heard it click; it was unreliable.

"Goddamn this cat," she said. She got down beside the bed and reached for Sheba, who shifted like running water out of reach. Ward said nothing. Laura got up and walked to the other side of the bed. "Goddamn you," she said, louder, to Sheba, who by then was sitting, compact and terrified, on the original side of the bed, pressed against the wall. Her worst fears had come to pass: her one true friend was trying to kill her. She placed her tail trimly over her feet.

"Sheba," hissed Laura, grabbing at her. The cat was too far away for her to reach.

Ward sighed. "What is it?" Laura told him, swearing. "Oh, Christ," he said.

Laura grabbed again for Sheba, but no matter which side she knelt on the cat was on the other with a swift, fearful patter. Laura could not bring herself to pretend friendship. She swore again, louder. The bed was too low for her to slide under; she could not get her head under it. Dust balls were everywhere beneath it. She shoved the frame, trying to fit beneath it, her body sprawled on the rug at Ward's feet. She pushed her head against it, like a pig, she thought, pushing forever, at twenty-three. But I love Wife. It's Wife I love."

Laura was twenty. It did not occur to her that she could say no. It was, after all, his decision, wasn't it? And besides, she didn't want to sound prudish. The sexual revolution swirled around them like guerrilla warfare, libidinal attacks in the streets, the subways, the singles bars. Then there was Nat's beguiling honesty, and the fact that he loved her. Somehow he made her a partner in all this; it was a weakness that she permitted him to indulge. And there was, besides, the fact that he made her laugh. Nat had always made her laugh, from the first night they had spent together.

They had gone out to dinner, and come back to Nat's for a drink. Around midnight, not sure of what Nat would do, and not sure of what she wanted him to do, Laura announced it was time for her to go home.

Nat shook his head solemnly. "Not possible, I'm afraid," he said. "I can't take you home."

"Why not?" Laura asked, nervous.

"I've already taken off my shoes."

Laura's first boyfriend had been handsome, dour and unresponsive. Nat was her second. She thought she had discovered something unique in the world: a friendly man. She married him.

After three years of Nat's guilty, delighted confessions, he and Laura lay in bed one night, companionably reading. Laura turned to him and said suddenly: "If I were any other woman in the whole world, lying here, you'd want to make love to me!" She made it funny, she used a voice of comic outrage. Nat laughed and patted her thigh. "I guess you're right," he said, and went on reading. Laura began an affair with her photography teacher.

Kenneth did not make her laugh, but Laura felt, when he looked at her, as though she were wholly, wholly visible, as though she were realer than anything. She could not get enough of this, the sense of absolute reality for him. It was like a drug. She felt, during the time she spent with Kenneth, like the filament in a lamp: glowing, radiant, trembling with energy, visible and necessary.

She hated having an affair. She hated lying. She hated coming home late, reeking of sex and guilt. She waited for it to be over. She felt that it existed in some sort of moral parenthesis, that soon it would be over, and once it were over it would never have existed. Often she broke it off. Each time, she would come across Nat's excited, roguish grin, and realize that he had another confession. Each time she went back to Kenneth. But she felt there was a slow poison tap dripping on her marriage.

In the summer Kenneth went to Europe. Laura grew careless, with only Nat to love her. When she discovered, to her horror, that she was pregnant, it seemed the end of everything. Did she really mean to spend her whole, whole life with Nat? She saw at once she had never meant it: now she had no choice. She could not imagine an abortion. Nat was thrilled.

Her first depression was overtaken by her body. Moving into pregnancy, she found herself sinking deeper and deeper into its life. She had abandoned her affair with Kenneth at once, fleeing from it as from a brilliant shameful dream. Now, as her body proceeded, the secret center of her at its mysterious work, she felt the external world fall away from her. Her marriage seemed less and less important: it would be merely a medium for her existence, the liquid in which she swam.

She woke often at night and lay with her eyes open in the dark, her hands resting on her rising belly. This would be the heart of things, now.

After Sammy was born, Laura and Nat had gone one night to a big party in Soho. Someone had bought a loft and was giving an open house. The loft was big and open and dark, with polished floors and big windows looking out onto the work. Nat was in Chicago, and it was the housekeeper's night off. Laura went straight in to Sammy's room, without taking off her coat, and sat on the bed. Sammy was sitting on the floor, sorting his letters. He had a can of them that he carried from room to room. He spent hours shifting them from one patch on the rug to another.

Laura spent the evening with him. The two of them sat together in the kitchen in white-painted Victorian chairs: Sammy's was a high chair, Laura's was a rocker. Laura sang to him while she fed him his dinner. Then they took a bath together in the tiny blue tub in Laura's bathroom. Sammy clambered onto her chest, his pink skin slippery against hers. They played hide-and-seek while Laura washed her hair for her lunch the next day.

The phone rang while she was in the tub. Dripping wet, her hair full of shampoo, Sammy alone in the tub, she stood freezing on the bedside rug and talked to Nat. It was a very brief conversation, and she did not have a chance to mention her lunch. She hurried back into the bathtub. Lunch is nothing, she told herself, sliding back into the warm, soapy water. Having lunch with someone is nothing at all. She turned on more hot water and slid down into it, submerging her shoulders.

The next day Laura walked in to the Oak Room bar fifteen minutes late. She did not want to risk being there first. If Ward were not there, she would leave. The ceilings were high, the woodwork dark oak, and all the men at the bar were strangers. She saw one of them wave, his hand held high. It was Ward, and Laura let out a sigh. She would stay, then.

As soon as they sat down, she said, "You know I'm married."

Ward smiled at her. "I know that. But I figured you could get off for lunch."

Laura leaned back and laughed, but she could not relax.

What she did not want was another affair. She was terrified of Ward. She did not want any touch of his; she did not want his shoe to touch hers by accident. He seemed very powerful to her: his size, his big golden head, his ease. She watched for him to be pompous; she watched for arrogance or conceit. But his gaze was clear and his manner mild; she found nothing.

He told her about himself: he had grown up in Chicago, the son of a Jewish furrier. His mother was a Unitarian from western Massachusetts. He had gone East to school—Andover, Columbia and Harvard Law. His father had sold the fur business and moved to Washington.

"He wants to play with the big guys," Ward said, smiling.

"Do you like him?"

"I love him," Ward said simply. Laura did not know men who said things like that.

"And you take photographs?" he had asked. "I have to warn you, I know nothing about photography."

"I mess around," Laura said, looking away.

She liked Ward. After lunch he walked her back to her office, without touching her. It was early spring, and the air felt light and reckless. They were in midtown, walking through the deep, windy spaces between skyscrapers, and, when they came out onto an open plaza at Park Avenue, the sky suddenly enlarged to a wild, brilliant span above her, and Laura felt giddy. She did not dare look at Ward now.

When she got back to her office, she sat down at her desk. Her office was a small, white cubicle, with a big window behind her and a huge cork board on the wall, covered with notes and pictures. She stared emptily at the board. She did not want another affair. She believed in a real marriage. Nat was the father of her child. He loved her. She knew that.

She was looking at a photograph on the board; it was black-and-white and had been taken in Ireland. It showed a long sweep of hillside covered with scrubby, thick grass. Along the ridge of the hill was a stone wall, old and patchworked. At one end of the wall was a stone farmhouse. Smoke came airily out of the chimney. A man carrying buckets was walking toward a shed behind the house, his sleeves rolled up, his pants stuffed into rubber boots. Above it was an enormous sky, enormous, with clouds shoving quickly past. What Laura liked about it was the idea of a life, a close, strong life in a vast empty landscape. She had wanted her marriage to be like that: intense, closed, and surrounded by wild space.

She turned her head away and looked out the window. Her view was chopped and quartered by tall buildings, some in sunlight, some in deep blue shadow. It was an odd, vertiginous landscape, the shadows cold, the sudden white spaces blazing. She could not seem to get a grip on it.

It was only lunch, Laura told herself, and he had not touched her.

They met for lunch every week. Ward did not touch her. He smiled at her and asked her about herself. Laura grew bold and told him.

"My father is the editor of the local paper," she said. "I grew up in the country outside Baltimore. My father is fierce. No drinking. No smoking. No consumerism. Everything on a very high moral plane."

"So you were way ahead of everyone in the sixties."

"Too far ahead. I'd grown up with all that stuff, while all my friends' parents drove Cadillacs and wore lipstick. My father wore thick sandals with socks. And we didn't have a TV set. I think we were the only family on the continent without a TV set. It was mortifying."

"So you rebelled?"

"How could I? All the rebels my age were doing just what I was trying to get away from. I went off to college and everyone was saying, 'Oh, wow, brown rice, pacifism, far out, man.' I wanted to throw up."

Ward laughed. "So no peace marches? No S.D.S.?"

Laura made a face. "I learned to *walk* on peace marches. I hated peace marches, and I hated social work. We always went off on work camps in the summers, to help the rural poor. At the work camps we ate margarine and powdered milk, and the women wore these saggy cotton dresses, and the men wore socks with their sandals. What I wanted was to be somewhere with a long, white beach. I wanted people who smoked cigarettes and let long drifts of blue come out of their open mouths. That's what I wanted. I *knew* I was wicked to feel that way. But that's what I wanted."

Ward laughed again. "So what did you do?"

"Nothing. I was a very good girl. I went to Sarah Lawrence. I met Nat and spent all my time at Princeton. He had a bright-red Jaguar. What I really wanted to get into was heavy drinking and real sex. And conspicuous consumption. That was my idea of heaven."

Ward laughed. She smiled back at him. She felt that he liked her. She knew he liked to look at her.

"And then what about you?" she asked, putting her chin on her hand.

"I'm just a lawyer," said Ward. "You know what they're like."

Laura shrugged. "Oh, yeah. Moral. Orderly. Competent. The usual."

"That's right."

"Are you really orderly? Do you hang up your clothes when you get home? Do you leave your socks on the rug?"

Ward looked her straight in the eye. "Clothes, yes. Socks, no. I mean I leave them on the rug."

"And? What happens to them? Are you married?" She was sure he was not, but as she asked she froze: what if he were?

He shook his head. "No. But I was."

"Oh, good," said Laura. "I mean, I have the feeling if you don't get married by a certain time, there's always something—I mean you get very difficult, set in your ways."

"Oh, I'm very difficult," said Ward.

She said nothing, wondering about his marriage.

"I was married for three years. We had a child. A daughter. She died. We split up."

"Oh, how terrible." Laura wished she had never asked.

Ward nodded. "It was terrible."

"Do you ever see her?"

"Not much. Once or twice a year. It was four years ago."

"I'm sorry." Laura looked down, embarrassed that she had made him talk about it.

"It was crib death. Now they call it SIDS—sudden infant death syndrome. They still don't know what causes it. Valerie went in to feed her, her milk woke her up. I heard her go in to the other room, and she usually talked to the baby, whispering, while she got her settled, nursing. I lay there listening, and I couldn't hear any sound at all. Then, after a long time, she came back in with the baby in her arms, and told me. She wouldn't let me hold it. She lay there for the rest of the night holding the baby."

"Oh, no," said Laura. She thought of Sammy, that she had somehow slipped through unscathed: a miracle.

"In the morning she let me hold the baby. She was so light. that was what struck me, she was so small, and light."

This expansion of Ward troubled Laura. She had not expected—she had not wanted—to see him as a lawyer, as a father. He was someone she could not take lightly.

Weeks later, walking behind her out of a restaurant through a dark hallway to the street, Ward had leaned forward, held her by the shoulders, and kissed the back of her neck. The shock of it was extraordinary. Laura felt ambushed in the sudden darkness, the brief solitude, of the hallway. His hands felt certain of her; he had taken hold of her absolutely. She felt his breath in the long tendrils sof her hair at the base of her neck; she felt his mouth moving along the tender skin there, slowly, as though he would take his time with her. She thought she could not breathe. She would have stumbled if he had not held her so tightly. It was as sharp as a hiss of breath. He released her arms, and she shook her hair back from her face and walked on.

After that he did not touch her again, but she knew that he could. When she looked up during a conversation and saw him watching her, she knew he was waiting. She did not dare brush against him, slipping into her chair: the touch of him against the side of her hand sent a long slide of feeling up into her. She did not dare touch him, and there were times, when he looked at her, that she did not dare look back.

She was not in love with him. She told herself that. But what she had to admit to herself was that, though she was not betraying Nat by sleeping with Ward, still he was being betrayed. She was moving away from him; she was searching. She could feel it, and she did not admit what it meant. She believed in marriage, she told herself, and Nat was the father of her child. But she had lunch with Ward every week, sometimes twice, washing her hair carefully each night before.

Once he said, touching just the end of a strand, "You have such shiny hair. Your hair is always so clean," and Laura had laughed. Did he think she did not prepare for him?

When Sammy was eighteen months old, Laura was feeding him his breakfast one morning in the kitchen. Laura sat in the rocker, wearing a furry bathrobe. Sammy, in his pajamas with the cowboy hats on them, was in the high chair. In the room next to the kitchen, which was Nat's dressing room, Laura could hear Nat begin to swear. She could hear him very precisely, as she was meant to.

"Goddamnit," Nat said.

Laura scraped a spoonful of cereal from the dish and headed it toward Sammy.

"*Goddamnit*," Nat said again, louder.

Laura slipped the spoonful of cereal almost all the way into Sammy's mouth. As she reached the mouth he turned his head sideways, suddenly, like a bird, and the cereal went onto the side of his cheek, into his hair, some into his ear. Laura put down the dish and picked up the washcloth. A good deal of Sammy's breakfast was already on it. Laura smiled at Sammy. "Where is Sammy's breakfast?" she asked him. Sammy smiled, and shook his head vigorously. "In his ear," Laura told him.

Nat appeared in the doorway. "Where the hell is it?" he asked. Laura looked up at him, scooping another spoonful for Sammy.

"Where is what?"

"Where the hell is my wallet?" Nat asked angrily. "I can't find it. I can't find it anywhere." Laura started the spoonful again toward Sammy's mouth. "Goddamnit, it really makes me mad. I mean, apart from everything else that's in it, my driver's license, all my credit cards—oh, Jesus, somebody's probably charging a trip to the Greek islands, I just can't believe I've lost it—and there's a check in there I have to deposit. Christ." Nat ran his hand through his hair.

"I haven't seen it," said Laura. She scoopped up another spoonful of cereal.

Nat turned around, his hands on his hips. He kicked into the air. "Goddamnit," he said, "I *wish* I knew where it was. I really wish I knew where it was."

Nat took pride in his temper, as though it were a purebred dog he had raised.

Laura set the plate down and kissed Sammy's nose. "What suit were you wearing yesterday?" she asked.

"I've looked in the suit I was wearing yesterday," said Nat angrily. "I've looked *every*where."

Laura went into his dressing room. Clothes had been hurled onto the floor and thrown over chairs and the bureau. Ties littered the rug.

"*Hmm*," said Laura, "looks like a fairly thorough search in here." She looked in his top drawer and under some mail.

"I told you it's not in here," said Nat. "Oh, God, I can't believe I've lost it. I'd better call the credit card people right now." He did not move.

Laura went back into the kitchen, and gave Sam another kiss. "I'll be right back," she said. "You stay with him for a minute, would you?" Nat stood stiffly by the high chair while Laura went down the hall, her bathrobe flapping around her legs. Nat's raincoat was hanging on the coatrack. She put her hand inside the breast pocket and took out the wallet. She walked back in to the kitchen and handed it to Nat.

"Oh, did you find it? Oh, what a good wife you are," said Nat. He took it from her and hugged her lengthily, pressing her against his chest. Laura's nose was pushed into his suit. It smelt of cleaning fluid.

"Oh, little Wifey," Nat said, "what would I do without you?"

Unbidden, the thought appeared as whole and solid as an apple held in the hand: *You'll find out.*

It was the end of Laura's marriage.

The idea of leaving Nat became a constant presence in Laura's mind. She nursed it to herself until it took over, until the idea of leaving had more reality than the idea of her marriage, of their life together, until each day stood waiting to be counted off, until, finally, waiting was all she was doing. She moved further and further from him. Nat could feel her leaving, and pursued her.

One night in bed he held her, moving relentlessly onto her side of the mattress until she was stretched, frantic and unstable, along the very edge of the bed. He wrapped himself around her body, twining his legs around hers. She thought she would choke, she felt a rising frenzy in her legs like a lack of air, slowly seeping up toward her head, her lungs. She could not breathe. She lay still, then her legs jerked as in a spasm, she kicked and pulled away from him.

"What's the matter?" he asked, moving tenderly around her again.

"Nothing," said Laura, pulling the sheet down and twitching her shoulders restlessly. "I'm so hot." Nat had waited too long for this.

"Don't you want your husband hugging you and things?" Nat asked, nosing around her ear, her neck. "Don't you love your husband?"

How could he ask, Laura wondered. She heard herself answer him in the dark. "Yes," she said. She told herself it was her last lie.

Like an actress before a first night, she was veined with fear. How would she stand up against him when she told him? In the end, she abandoned all her careful plans, her debating tricks. Terrified of his response, she had seized emotion as her own tool, leaving him with rationality. She had been hysterical. She knew this was cowardly and unfair, but she was afraid of what would happen if she allowed Nat to start in on how he felt. She had given him no opening; she had given him no choice but to be the grown-up—calm, rational, comforting. And to her surprise, he had been steady and sensible. Secretly, Laura admired this; it did not alter her purpose. By now she had something large to sustain her, something besides her marriage—the conviction that it was over, and she held on to that with a deadly grip.

But this was not what she had ever wanted, divorce. What she wanted was romance, a happy ending. Nat was the father of her child. After she had told Nat he must leave the house, she grieved, waiting for him to convince her she had been wrong, that things between them could be righted. Nat called her often, using a strange, gentle voice she did not know. He appeared on the doorsill, to collect his mail, to see Sammy, unhappiness hung around him like a cloak. He did not reproach her. He took her to dinner, small, modest places.

Subdued, he promised her things, he pointed things out to her, he recalled things that should have swayed her, that should have brought her suddenly to her senses. But behind it Laura could see no change from the man who had destroyed the antique coffee table the ushers had sent them for a wedding present, battering at it with a hammer because he could not get the heavy packing crate off it; the man who got the long slow smiles from the girls who flew the red-eye from Los Angeles.

While she listened to Nat, miserable, things bumped awkwardly along between their lawyers. Nat was reasonable. Laura signed her initials to twenty-eight Xeroxed pages that proved in the eyes of the law that she could find in her heart no love for her husband, and that she would no longer share his life. She wept as she signed, trying to disguise her sniffs as hiccups, and smearing the initials.

Nat called her the next day to tell her, to emphasize the fact, that the agreement was still only between the two of them, that at any time for a year they could, if they wished, simply tear it up, and it would be as though it had never been written. "Any time we want," he said, "we can tear it up."

Nine

Laura spent the afternoon cleaning out the linen closet. It was precisely the kind of job she needed: quiet, finite, sensible. She had reached the limit of her emotions. The situation downstairs was beyond her; she turned her attention toward restoring order in the linen closet. She carried pile after pile of the fouled sheets down to the laundry room. This was a dreary place, with dark-green walls and a concrete floor; it had been built for servants, and not favorite servants.

Laura had found Sheba in a closet. They had not discussed Sheba's crime. Laura had carried her gently downstairs, the velvet limbs rigid with alarm, and let her go in the laundry room. The cat leapt stiffly onto the floor and hurried toward the wall, her body low to the ground in a flattened trot. When she reached the wall, Sheba did not stop but flowed along it until she reached more shelter, the unpainted metal legs of the old wash tubs. Here Sheba curled up, her tail neatly covering her front feet, in case that might help. The Kitty Litter box was on the other side of the room, near the door outside, but, when Sheba's head turned in that direction, her golden gaze passed through it like sunlight through a pane of glass. She did not admit its meaning.

Laura made a sign for the door: PLEASE DO NOT LET THE CAT OUT. She went back upstairs with a bucket of soapy water and ammonia to start on the shelves. The acid smell of the ammonia was a relief to her. She scrubbed fiercely at the shelves.

Pia came and stood in the hallway, her short curve of blond hair bright in the sunlight. She swayed back and forth, hands in her blue jean pockets, balancing on the balls of her bare feet. She said nothing.

"Hello," Laura said finally. "Want to help?"

Pia nodded, pleased.

She saw her aunt as glamorous, a city woman, rich and temperamental. Pia herself would not have dared temperament. She knelt and took a sponge, rubbing at a darkened patch on the wood.

"Pew," she said, "this *really* stinks."

Laura scrubbed, two shelves above her. "We weren't allowed to use that word. When we were little."

"Pew?"

"Stinks."

"Stinks," repeated Pia, testing the newly important word. "I like it. It sounds like just what it means."

"It does," agreed Laura.

Three times she made the long trip downstairs to the laundry room, changing loads of sheets, refilling the bucket.

"Clean water," she told Pia, "that's the most important thing."

"Do you like to clean?"

"I don't do it much," said Laura, "so I don't mind it."

"Yeah," said Pia. "We do our own."

"I did my own when I was your age," offered Laura, as though freedom from cleaning was something she had earned with age, instead of through marrying rich.

"Well, I hate it," announced Pia, who then wondered if she sounded rude. "But I don't mind this."

"It's always more fun to work in a strange house."

"But what do you do, then?" asked Pia suddenly, as though, without housecleaning, Laura's day must stretch blank and unrelieved before her.

"I'm a photographer," said Laura, turning stiff.

"But what do you do? In the morning."

"Different things," said Laura, tightening with guilt. There were mornings, there were days, weeks, when she did nothing concerned with photography.

"But do you take pictures every day?" persisted Pia.

"Sometimes. Sometimes I develop them in the darkroom. Sometimes I don't do either."

There was a pause.

"Where do your pictures come out?"

"Different places," said Laura. She squeezed out her sponge. "This stuff is strong. I can't tell if the smell is cat or ammonia; it seems to be the same."

Pia said nothing, and Laura relented, embarrassed.

"I'm not famous, you know," she said. "Lots of times my pictures don't come out anywhere. One of the things I have to do besides photograph is take the stuff around and show it to people, you know, from magazines and museums and things, hoping that they'll like and use it."

Pia's voice expressed horror. "You have to *take* it to them? Yourself?" Laura nodded. "How awful!" she said, reveling in the awfulness. "And stand there and have them not like it? How awful!"

"Something like that," said Laura disarmed. She was trying to keep above Pia. She did not imagine Pia's admiration for her.

"Why don't you do something else?" suggested Pia.

"What?"

"You could teach. You could teach photography."

"I don't really like the idea of being tied down to a rigid schedule," said Laura. She could not afford to take advice from a child. And there were other things: *could* she teach? She was afraid to venture too far out into life; a job seemed in the middle of the white water: she might capsize, she might easily drown. "And then there's Sammy," she went on, gaining authority. "He comes home at two-thirty every day. Two-thirty to five-thirty or six is a long time for a young child. Every day." The image of the child was before her, pathetic: motionless, saddened, he stood before a window, transformed by her desertion, his life suspended until her return.

"If my mother left me alone every afternoon—" said Pia, and paused. Laura waited, feeling noble. Motherhood meant sacrifice.

"—I'd *love* it," Pia finished, feelingly. Before her was another image: herself alone, supreme in the silent house, the boards sounding only beneath her feet, the doors moving only to her touch, the afternoon stretched quiet and inviting before her, hers to arrange, to command.

Laura laughed.

Still, Laura did not allow herself to slip past her guilt. Sacrifice was what she understood, believed.

"Sammy's much younger than you," she told Pia. "He needs a lot of looking after. And there's only me."

"There's Ward," offered Pia.

"Ward," said Laura, without agreeing. She did not trust Ward with Sam: she feared the day when he resented another man's child in his house. She kept Sammy from him when she could, never asking him to take responsibility.

Pia heard her dissent. "Doesn't Ward have his own children?"

"No. There was one but it died."

"How awful." Pia was at the age when worldly horror becomes acutely embarrassing, tragedy is perceivable but unconvincing. When Pia heard something terrible, she was apt, unsuitably, to smile uncontrollably. "How did it die?" she asked, keeping her head down in case the smile made an appearance.

"Crib death," said Laura, "no one knows. They found it in the night."

"Without a mark on its body," finished Pia without meaning to. "I mean, how terrible," she added quickly.

"Yes," said Laura. The story made her uncomfortable: how might things have been different between Ward and Valerie had that small corpse not lain before them, producing, by extinction of its own life, a tide of unexplained guilt that washed the shore of each of them, separating and connecting them forever?

The afternoon had slipped gently back from them; the water had receded from the stony beachline below the house. The upstairs hall—flooded with light when they began and looking as though any of the paneled wooden doors might have opened suddenly to a brisk hand, the sunshot air have supported any voice—now began to look visibly unpeopled, the shadows strengthening, masking the doorways and making conversation improbable. Laura looked at her watch.

"Now. It's late. We're about done, I'd say. What do you think?"

Pia stood aside, waiting for her aunt's pronouncement.

Laura sniffed along the shelves. "Not bad," she said. "Let's stop. We'll give it another sniff in the morning."

They carried the things downstairs. In the laundry room Laura shifted loads again. She looked around for Sheba but it was Pia who found her, pressed against the dryer.

"She likes the heat," said Pia, stroking her. "I'll bring her some food."

"Good," said Laura. With the light, the heat and the piles of clean white sheets the laundry room had been transformed. It was now a pleasant place, warm and comforting. Two big hanging lights flared a pool of brightness across the floor.

Laura stood over the big zinc-topped table, folding sheets, restoring order. She had stopped thinking about dinner and her sins against Ward. Finishing the pile, she stooped to stroke the cat. Sheba gazed mildly at her, her tail curled tightly around her rump. Laura went upstairs to Ward.

He was still working on the bed, his face close to the papers in the dusky light. Laura sat down near him.

"How's it coming?" she asked.

"Nearly done," he said. "How about you?"

"Everything's clean. Pia helped me."

"That's nice," Ward said. She sat close to him, hoping that the sense of her, even if he would not look up at her, would remind him of the facts: there she was, warm and human. The weight of her on the mattress made him shift, his muscles tightening against her presence. He did not look up at her.

"Do you want the shower first?" He shook his head. "I'll use it, then, and go down and help Sarah."

She stood up and waited, but he did not answer. She left the room, pretending they were friends.

Ten

They all sat at the same table at dinner. Sarah had roasted a big ham smeared with mustard and brown sugar, and there were sweet corn and green beans. Sarah raised her glass.

"Here's to us all being here," she said bravely.

Nathaniel assumed the toast was meant for him, and answered her. "Here's to being here," he said.

"Very nice," said Richie obscurely, and Ward and Laura drank without comment.

"This ham is delicious," said Nat politely.

"Disgusting," Karin corrected him.

"Would you like some more sauce on it?" Sarah asked quickly. But Nat had heard Karin. He liked outrageousness.

"Delicious," he repeated. "What you're eating is disgusting. Toe-cheese."

"What you're eating is murdered pig meat," said Karin. She did not expect a grown-up to argue with her.

"Toe-cheese!" said Pia, delighted.

"Shut up, Vomit," said Karin.

"What you're eating is murdered lettuce," said Nat. "Little trusting things, thrusting up their soft, little leaves, their soft little heads, trusting that kind gardener, believing in him—Chop chop. The Big Knife."

Karin looked at her plate to keep from smiling. "Plants have no feelings," she said severely; "they have no brains."

"Sounds like intellectual snobbery to me," said Nat. "You think because somebody's not very smart they don't care if they're killed? What about chickens? They're just about as smart as lettuce." There was a pause. "Maybe lettuce is a bit smarter," Nat amended.

Karin glared at him. "You are *so* out of it," she said scornfully.

"What about *The Secret Life of Plants*? Didn't you ever read that? If you tell your plants you love them they put out new leaves. One quarrel and they go into shock. Feelings! All organic life has feelings."

Karin said nothing, eating tofu in very small bites.

"Toe-cheese," said Pia solemnly. Karin gave her a look of grave disgust.

"How do you know about *The Secret Life of Plants*?" asked Laura suspiciously. "You don't read books."

"I read a lot now," said Nat cheerfully. "You missed a bet. I might turn out to be quite civilized."

"Reading about the emotions of cucumbers is hardly going to qualify you for civilization," said Laura, "though it's a start, I admit."

Karin laughed quietly, pleased to have someone else take over as target.

"Now, now," said Nat, laughing. He liked this. He was beginning to feel like a member of the family.

"I was on Cadillac Mountain this afternoon," said Richie. "I saw the Outward Bounders."

"What were they doing?" asked Sarah.

"They were swimming," said Richie; "it was freezing."

"If I were in Outward Bound," said Nat, "I'd hire someone to do the stuff for me."

"It does seem strange to pay for physical duress," said Sarah.

"But don't you think it sounds fun, in a weird way?" asked Laura.

"I'd rather do it on my own," said Sarah.

"You do, babe, you do," said Richie. "Life with Sarah *is* Outward Bound." He turned to Ward. "You missed her swimming excursion while you were gone. She went across the harbor and back. It took four hours to recover: blankets, hot water bottles, long johns, the works." Sarah smiled, pleased.

"I don't see the point of swimming in freezing water," said Laura.

"I don't mean there to be a point," said Sarah, "I just like it."

"Sarah's not really happy unless she's miserable," said Richie. Nat passed him the wine to refill his glass.

"I'm not happy being miserable, I just happen to like some things you don't," said Sarah.

"Like margarine," said Laura, and wished she hadn't.

"Everyone likes something different," said Pia. "Karin likes toe-cheese, for example."

There was a silence. Everyone feared they had gone too far. Richie refilled wine glasses, and set the bottle down in front of Ward.

"Well, I do like swimming in cold water," said Sarah, as though that had been in question.

"We know you do, babe," Richie said not quite kindly.

"Your mother," began Laura to Pia, "is a bit nuts." On her second glass of wine she was becoming expansive. She tapped her forehead at Karin, who smiled but twitched her head away, unwilling to take sides.

"I, on the other hand," said Laura, waving her hand in a queenly manner, "loathe swimming in cold water. I loathe it. I always pretended to like it when Sarah and Father went swimming in the Alps, but the truth can now be told I loathed it. I am purely self-indulgent, and I really only like being in hot water."

"You're in it most of the time" said Ward, but she did not seem to hear him.

"*Very* hot water," Laura went on; "the very the hotter." She giggled.

"Well, I like hot baths, too," said Sarah. She picked up a platter. "Who wants seconds?"

"So does Vomit," said Karin. "That's Vomit's only indoor sport, using up all the hot water."

"Karin," said Richie. His voice had an edge to it.

"Hey, that's great," said Nat. "Nice to see you two girls getting along so well." He helped himself to seconds.

Laura went to change a load of sheets from washer to dryer. When she turned on the dryer, it thumped heavily, and, exasperated, she waited to see if it would stop. But it droned on, still thumping, and she went back to the dining room. "Sheba's in the laundry room. Nobody let her out."

"Right," said Nat responsibly, finishing his wine. Sarah rose and went into the kitchen to make coffee.

Nat raised his empty wine glass and looked around. There was an open bottle in front of Ward. Nat looked inquiringly at him. Ward stared at him and did not move.

"Ward?" said Nat terribly politely.

"Yes?"

"Do you think, could I possibly have a little of that vino in front of you?"

Without speaking, Ward held up the bottle and Nat held out his glass. Ward filled it. He did not look at Nat's face. There was a silence while Nat drank.

"Well, Kareen," said Ward, using the family nickname for her, "I hear you saw *Casablanca*."

"Yeah," said Karin.

"What did you think?"

"Excellent," said Karin; "really good."

"What did you like about it?" asked Nat, leaning on his elbows. He wanted to be the center. Ward looked away.

"It was so romantic," said Karin, turning to Nat. "Like at the end, when she walks toward the airplane and then you realize Rick is going to stay—" Karin clasped her hands and put them to her chest, making a face of pathos.

"My darling," supplied Pia.

"Oh, shut up, Vomit," said Karin, her face normal.

"*Vomit is you*," shrieked Pia, beside herself. "Didn't you know that?" There was something lacking in the things she said to Karin, Pia could feel that. Karin had a smooth and classy tone Pia could not manage.

"Karin," said Richie, "do not call Pia 'Vomit.' "

Karin shrugged and did not look at him.

"This is great," said Nat nodding and smiling. "Tell me, have you two girls always been so close?"

Everyone laughed. He did that often, Laura remembered, make people laugh, and she remembered loving him. Stirred by the wine, she hoped he remembered loving her. She hoped everyone loved her.

"Actually," said Sarah, laughing, "this is nothing. When you have teenage daughters, Nat, you will know that this is nothing."

"Actually," said Nat, "I think the chances of my having teenage daughters is fairly slim."

"You see, girls, what effect you have? Who could blame the man, after watching you two?" said Richie.

"If she's a teenager, then I resign from the category," said Karin.

"I can see why you don't eat pork, Karin," said Pia. "You don't want to be a cannibal."

"Ha. Ha. Ha," said Karin.

There was a pause. Nat began again.

"No, it's not that, I mean just generally I think there's very little chance of my having teenage daughters."

Laura could see that Nat had in his mind an image of abandonment, as she had earlier had one of Sam. The figure in Nat's mind was himself: forlorn and bereft, awash in a foamy sea of self-pity, his life halted.

"That's a perfectly asinine thing to say," said Laura. "Unless you're planning on an operation."

"No," said Nat, shaking his head. "No operation. It is just what I imagine."

"You're such an ass," said Laura.

Nat gave a false laugh.

"Stop it," said Ward.

"He is an ass," said Laura. "He wants us all to think poor Nat, his life was ruined by his terrible wife."

"Stop it," Ward said again.

"I'll stop if he stops," said Laura.

"You asked him here," said Ward. "I presume you didn't do that to humiliate him at the dinner table."

"What do you mean?" asked Laura. "What are you saying?"

"Why did you ask him here?" asked Ward.

"I thought perhaps he might be allowed to see his son," Laura said coldly.

"He can see his son. Why did you ask him here?"

"I don't know what you're talking about," said Laura.

"You want it both ways," said Ward. No one else at the table moved. "You can't have it both ways. You left Nat, Laura, that is what you did. You can't make it up to him by asking him to my house for the weekend."

"Don't be so pompous," said Laura, afraid he was right.

"You want everyone to love you. You don't want to take responsibility for anything unpleasant."

"Now look," said Nat sententiously, "let's not blame Laura for everything. I probably shouldn't have come up here. I probably shouldn't. Blame me for it, not Laura.

"I do," said Ward.

"Okay," said Nat, shrugging his shoulders, his eyes hooded, "do."

"I just told you that I do. You should not have come here!" Ward's voice was raised.

"I came here as Laura's guest," said Nat, shifting ground. "I am Laura's guest in this house."

"Laura is my guest in this house!" said Ward, his eyes terrible. He stood up. There was a pause. Nat folded his arms across his chest and stared at him, arrogant. Sammy upset his milk.

"I upset my milk," he announced, fearful. "It's on my legs." It was on his legs, it was on the floor, it ran smoothly along the table, sopping napkins and surrounding plates. Pia and Sarah both jumped up to clean it. Laura sat still. Sammy's eyes were huge; they were like Sheba's, Laura thought.

"You blame everyone," said Laura to Ward. "Everyone is wrong but you."

"No," said Ward. He looked at her steadily. "I was wrong about you."

Laura felt quite calm. "Oh?" she said. "And what did you think I was like? Did you think I was like Sarah? Did you think that I was going to bake my own bread and knit all your sweaters?"

Ward shook his head. "It never occurred to me that you would bake bread or knit sweaters. But I thought, when I met you, that the desolation around you was not your fault."

There was silence. Laura waited for him to go on. She hated him. He said nothing.

"And so?" she said, tilting her head back.

"I can't fight with you," said Ward. "If you want to destroy things, I can't stop you."

There was another silence. Laura took a slow drink of her wine.

Nat could not bear to be left out of things. "I wouldn't

say it was really Laura's fault that our marriage fell apart," he said.

Ward looked at him and shook his head. "What amazes me about you is how little idea of other people's feelings you have." They stared at each other. "Don't you think, now, that this is not a conversation for you to enter?"

Nat crossed his arms on his chest. Now he was getting angry. "You aren't exactly in the privacy of your boudoir. This is a public conversation, and it concerns my wife, and my marriage. I see no reason for me not to enter it."

"Calling Laura your wife is hardly appropriate at the moment." said Ward.

"She is actually my wife," said Nat.

Laura watched them both. She could not imagine what they were talking about. What were they doing? She was trying to fight off Ward's words. Why was *Nat* so angry? He had pushed his chair away from the table and had crossed his leg at the knee, tilting back in the chair.

"Nat," said Sarah softly, putting her hand out toward him. He looked at her and she smiled. "Don't tilt back in these chairs, do you mind? They're kind of rickety."

Sarah was right, thought Laura wildly, they were rickety, these chairs. They were really rickety, old kitchen-Windsors, painted blue, and it was nothing but foolish for Nat to lean back in them. She did not want to look at Sammy.

Pia stood up, her head down, and began clearing the table. Karin did the same, cowed, for once, by grown-ups.

Ward stood up and left the room. Laura wondered if he were going to bed, if he wanted her to follow, if he wanted her at all. I hate him, she thought. She wished he had told her to come up with him.

She wondered where she would go, and if she would take Sammy. What she wanted to do was to sweep grandly out, but Ward would not even see it if she did. And she did not want to leave without Sammy, and she could not bear the fact that Sammy had seen all this. Sammy had heard what Ward had said. Children were supposed to think that their parents created peace, that mothers were there to mend and soothe. She could not face Sammy.

She finished the wine in her glass again and stood up, slightly unsteadily. At least she would put the last load of sheets in the dryer.

She went into the laundry room, closing the door carefully behind her. She did not see Sheba anywhere. She knelt on the floor, peering under the tables. There was no sign of Sheba. Laura called her, and waited for the cat to appear, a soft, dim figure tiptoeing across the floor, her tail high, curling gently at the tip. But Sheba stayed hidden, wherever she was. Laura stood up at last and opened the dryer to take out the dry sheets. They were not clean. There was blood on them: a trail of dark drops, pooled in places. Laura's first, illogical, thought was that the sheets had gone through the washer and the dryer like that, but of course that was impossible. She pulled more of them out and found that something heavy was holding them in place. The blood was from Sheba, whose neck had been broken by the first revolutions of the steel drum inside the machine. The cat lay at the bottom of the dryer, her nose and mouth a sticky mask of blood.

Laura sat down on the floor and took the cat in her lap. She arranged Sheba's body as though she were sleeping. She began to stroke the fur of the cat, which was no longer sleek. Laura could not make it smooth. Everything she touched, thought Laura. She wondered what would be next.

Eleven

If Ward was awake when Laura came up, he did not show it. He did not move or speak as she got into bed. Laura arranged herself carefully, without touching him. Silently, she let out her breath when she was settled. The room was very dark. The window was a deep-blue square, she could see no stars. Laura could hear the hum of the electric clock, and after a while she could hear Ward's breathing. She imagined the rise of his big chest, she thought of his ribs widening in an arc as air flowed into him. The room seemed very big, bigger than it did in daylight. Laura lay very still, as though to minimize herself.

Ward rolled over on his side, facing her. Usually, as he slept his body reached out for her, his ankle crossing hers, an arm flung around her, and often, when he rolled over, his body closed around hers, his front pressing against the length of her back. Tonight he did not touch her. Disappointed, she rolled over too, away from him. She had thought that, asleep, even though he was angry, his body might seek its solace in her own, but the anger had penetrated his sleep, and his body was remote and aloof as a stranger's.

Facing away from him, she could not hear his breathing. Perhaps he was not breathing. Perhaps he was, like her, holding his breath, listening for her breathing. Though she longed to, nothing in the world would have made Laura reach out and touch Ward in the dark. She raised her head slightly, unmuffling her ear from the pillow, and could then hear the gentle soughing of Ward's breath.

Her eyes had become accustomed to the dark, and she could make out the heavy shapes of the pine branches against the night sky. Laura listened to the harbor sounds, the faint slip of the water against the rocks, the quiet clinking of stays and pulleys. She had never felt so bad.

"Ward?" she finally whispered. She could not bear her thoughts anymore, they took her in a long, sweeping spiral down. Ward did not answer, but she could not lie there alone. "Ward?" she whispered again. Though why was she whispering, she wondered; she was, after all, trying to wake him.

"What is it?" Ward answered. His voice was clear and distant. He could not have been asleep. Now that he had answered, she hesitated. She had nothing to say. She was locked inside a wall of misery, trapped inside a searching self-hatred that made it difficult for her to see other people at all. She had nothing to say, she wanted only to make contact.

"What is it?" Ward asked again, his voice unfriendly.

"I suppose you blame me for everything," Laura said challengingly. She wanted someone to attack besides herself.

Ward did not turn over. "I blame you for what you've done."

Laura blamed herself for everything. "Oh, I see," she said fiercely. "But you, of course, have done nothing. You're never to blame for anything."

Ward rolled over. "I try to live my life responsibly."

"Don't be such a prig," Laura said rudely.

"I'm not being a prig," Ward said. "I do try to behave responsibly."

"*Do* you," said Laura. "It was very responsible to start an affair with a married woman, wasn't it. Very high-minded and responsible. I wonder how Nat feels about your idea of responsibility?"

Ward snorted. "Go to sleep," he said. "Don't waste your craziness on me. Save it for Nat; he could work it up into something terrific. The two of you were made for each other."

"Is that what you think?" Laura leaned up on her elbow. "Is that what you really think?" It was, she thought; that was just what Ward thought. He held Nat in complete contempt, and he thought she was just like him. He thought she was not quite up to his own standards, not quite good enough, somehow.

"I'm not crazy, you know," she said firmly. In fact, she was sure she was crazy; it was a relief to think she was crazy: a justification for the horror inside her head, for the terrible things she did.

Ward laughed. "Oh, no, you're not crazy," he said. "What about the time you threw the pork chops at me?"

"I didn't throw them at you. I didn't come anywhere close to hitting you with those pork chops," Laura said scornfully, "and you know that perfectly well."

"Right," said Ward, "you were aiming for that empty space on the wall between the mirror and the bookcase. They looked great there, briefly."

Laura did not answer.

"And what about throwing the bottle of wine out the window? Six floors up?"

"I didn't hit anyone," Laura said uncomfortably. She had to admit, that had been a stupid thing to do. She and Ward had stared at each other, paralyzed, as the bottle fell, waiting for the sound of it smashing only against the sidewalk, hoping for no human cry. What she had wanted was a gesture, a grand distraction. She had never meant to hurt anyone.

"You're crazy as a stoat," Ward said dismissively. "You've gone too far this time. It's not worth it. You go too far."

Laura closed her eyes. This was what she had been waiting for, for months; since she had met him, she had known Ward would do this. "You say that," she said; "you're as crazy as I am. You want to control everything, you want to control the world. You can't keep things nice and smooth and even, either."

Ward laughed in a superior way. He rolled onto his back. "Not with you around. Remember when you pulled the whole mattress onto the floor trying to get me out of my own bed?"

"Things get away from you, too, Ward," Laura said.

"Oh?" Ward's voice was contemptuous.

"What about your marriage. What about your walking out on Valerie? How responsible was that? What about your baby dying? Was that what you planned?"

Ward sat up in bed and slapped Laura in the face. The shock of it was intense; the hollow structure of her skull rang. Tears came to her eyes, and there was an echoing vibration in her ears. She had been assaulted; her most central self had been attacked. She and Ward stared at each other.

"I knew you were like that," she said carefully, keeping the tremble away from her voice. She had this against him; she would have it forever. She lay back down, her back turned to Ward. He did not move.

"Damn you," he said. He made it sound deadly.

Laura put her cheek carefully on the pillow. Her cheek stung, and she moved her face tenderly on the pillowcase. Ward had hit her quite hard. He had finally declared himself. She felt somehow virtuous, triumphant. She would never forgive him for this, never. She began to shake. Her teeth began to chatter. Ward lay silent and still. He was gone from her. He would not be back. It was over. Laura began to cry, silently. Ward did not move.

Finally, Laura sat up in bed. "I hate you," she whispered.

"Evidently," said Ward.

"You shit," Laura said. She raised her pillow and brought it down on his head as hard as she could, not like a child but like a murderer. "You're such a shit."

Ward threw the pillow away from him. "And you're just a sweet little thing who's too confused to know what she's saying?"

"You're such a shit," Laura said. She raised her face to the ceiling. The tears ran down her temples and into her hair. "I hate you," she said again.

"Well, you've made that very clear, in your own adorable way," Ward said. "You think you have license to say anything you want because you're crazy. Well, if you're crazy, then you should be treated like a crazy; you should go live with other crazies. If you want to be treated like a normal person, then you should know you have no more license than anyone else."

"You asshole," said Laura, crying.

"You think you can have everything. You think you can walk out on Nat, move in with me, drag poor old Nat back into things, ask him up for the weekend, be sweet to him, mean to me, sweet to me, mean to him, and everyone will still think you're just a darling, flutter-brained sweetheart. Well, at some point they won't." Ward's voice was stony. "You have all the excuses for yourself; you think you can excuse everything. You don't want to get a job, you don't want to get married, you don't want to get divorced. You don't dare take a stand on anything; someone might disagree with you, someone might get mad at you. You don't dare take your photography seriously; someone might not like your pictures. You're such a coward; you're so goddamned terrified of failure you don't dare do a goddamned thing."

Laura put her fingers over her eyes. The words fell into her mind like stone. What he was saying was true. It was not something she could listen to, and she shook her head, meaning for him to stop.

"You can't stand to have me say it, can you?" asked Ward. He leaned over her, huge and black in the dark room. "You can't stand anything, you can't face anything. What a shit I am, for saying these terrible things to you. I'm surprised you don't slap *me* in the face." He moved closer. Laura took her hands away from her face. "Go on," said Ward, "why don't you?"

Laura did. She slapped him in the face as hard as she could. There was a long silence. Laura's hand hurt, and she squeezed the fingers with her other hand. Ward did not speak. Laura held her breath.

Ward got out of bed deliberately. He went into the bathroom. He didn't shut the door, and Laura listened, still holding her breath. She heard the steady sound of him peeing. The sound was distant and private, and it frightened Laura. His life had nothing to do with her, then. He would go on without her. What he did, all his private thoughts, his gestures, were his own. She would not be a part of him. She heard him run the water, and she pictured him drinking, standing alone in the dark, his chin raised, his throat long and pure, the cool water becoming part of him: she had nothing to do with any of it.

She wondered if he would come back and lie beside her. Perhaps he would leave right now; perhaps he would just get dressed right now and take the car and go to the airport, and that would be the end of it. What would she say to everyone in the morning? How would she explain? And then how would she arrange her life, all the rest of it?

Ward came back into the bedroom and lay down on the bed as though there were no one else in it, and yanked the sheet back up again, over his shoulders, covering himself. He did not speak to Laura. After a while Laura lay back down again, too, arranging her tender cheek against the pillow. They were facing away from each other. It was over between them; this was final.

In the morning Laura had cramps in her legs from keeping them tucked in her corner of the bed all night. She opened her eyes without moving. She was still facing the window, and the sky outside was a dull gray. She heard Ward behind her. He stretched out, spread-eagling on the bed. He did not touch her. She heard him rub his face to wake it up. Laura did not move.

"Well?" said Ward, rubbing his fists into his eyes. "Now what?" He gave a sudden rush of a yawn.

"What do you mean?" Laura asked distantly.

Ward spread his arms out. His hand touched her shoulder and Laura flinched, as though she expected to be hit. Ward's hand, touching her by accident, curved around her shoulder by reflex. His hand, his flesh, was amazingly warm. Laura yearned for it. What, she wondered, if she turned and yielded to that warmth, let herself be smoothed and curved? But she lay still, determined. Things had gone too far last night for easy reconciliations. Laura viewed softening as weakness; she took pride in her own resoluteness.

"What is it that you want?" Ward asked.

"Nothing new," said Laura, countering. Why should she answer him? He was her true enemy.

Ward sighed. "This gets me down, Laura." he said. His voice was quiet and heavy. "I don't know what you want. I really don't. I'm not going to stay around for much more of this. I just don't think you know what you're doing. Or maybe you do. Maybe you're doing all this on purpose."

Laura spoke without turning to him. "I'm sorry I slapped you," she said coldly. She had apologized first, anyway.

"I'm sorry I slapped *you*," Ward said politely, but his hand left her shoulder, and his voice was cool. Just get *out*, Laura thought; everything is over, just get out and leave me alone.

When he sat up, his back to her, she rolled over to look at him. His bare back curved into a tired slump at the shoulders. Laura put out her hand almost touching his skin. She traced the line of his spine in the air, the smooth hard curves beneath the skin, from his neck down to the pale tip of it, in the shallow dip between his buttocks. She wanted Ward to turn to her, she wanted his warmth around her. She did not touch his skin.

"Well," Ward said, his back still to her, "another great day. I think I'll spend it at the tennis courts with Allen Cartwright. Unless you're planning to bring old Asshole up there for ex-spouse singles."

"What?"

"You know. Asshole."

"Don't call him Asshole," Laura said.

"Yeah, but he is," Ward said. "Drinking up all the wine, hitting those great poses, flirting with the nieces. Anyway, keep him away from the tennis courts. If you don't mind."

When Ward came out of the bathroom, dressed and shaved, Laura saw his full face for the first time. On his cheek was a curious red stain, deep under the skin.

"What's that?" she asked.

"I believe it's called contusions," Ward said.

"I did that?" Laura was shocked: she had hurt Ward. She had left a record of the damage she had done. "Oh, Ward," she said. She had not believed she could hurt him. But Ward's moment for intimacy, for forgiveness, was past, and he was distant from her, shaved, smooth, sleek, buttoned and clothed. He did not move toward her.

"See you later," he said, and left.

Twelve

When Laura came downstairs, Ward had already gone. The others were having breakfast; Sarah had made Swedish pancakes.

"Sheba is dead," Laura announced defiantly. When she told them what had happened, Sarah came over to her, the spoon still in her hand, and put her arm around her sister.

"How awful for you," she said.

"*Yee-uck*," said Karin, "in the dryer."

"Karin, for God's sake," said Richie.

Sammy asked to see the cat, and he and Laura crouched over the limp gray huddle and stroked the lifeless fur. After breakfast they buried her, on the steep slope between the house and the water. Laura stood and held Sammy's hand. Nat held his other hand. They watched Richie heave spadefuls of black dirt and rusty pine needles. When it was deep enough, Laura leaned over and put Sheba's body, in its shoe box, carefully into the hole. Unexpectedly, she began to cry, and stroked the small torso, curling the tail around Sheba's legs, as though she were cozy. Sammy looked frightened and began to sniff sympathetically.

"Poor Sheba," Nat said mournfully, catching it.

Richie said nothing, waiting for a moment before gently sliding earth and pine needles on top of the cat. There seemed to be more earth to put back than there had been to take out, and the grave was a small mound among the tree trunks. Nat and Richie together pulled a heavy chunk of granite over to mark it.

Afterward, Nat stood aimlessly on the front lawn with Sammy, as though he were waiting for Laura to take charge of him. She thought that if she had to talk to him she would scream.

"Why don't you take Sammy down to the beach?" she said. "I'll show you how to go and you can take sandwiches." Nat looked blank; he had hoped she would come with them. But her face did not change, so he smiled. "The beach would be terrific," he said politely. Laura stood in the front door and waved to Sammy when they left.

Richie came downstairs behind her, whistling. She moved aside and he paused outside on the doorstep. "Want to come?"

"Where?" Laura was not sure she could speak to anyone without screaming. On the other hand, if she stayed here, there was no telling how long the day would get to be, there was no telling that it would end, ever.

"I'm going to hike up to the old Rockefeller house, up above Seal Harbor, and watch the boats. You'd better come. Get away from it all."

He smiled, and she smiled back. "Okay," she said, relieved by the thought of being out in the air.

The weather had changed. That morning the sky had been gray and airless, sullen clouds had pushed past one another, but a strong southeast wind had blown this away, and the sky was now clear and high and transparent. The wind was steady, making the tops of the pine trees bend gracefully, and the tips of the waves turn foam-white.

They parked at the public beach and began the long walk up through the woods. "I've been here twice," said Richie, "but I'm still not sure of the way." The path was narrow and not clearly marked, and Laura concentrated on Richie's calves before her, his sneakered feet padding softly along the leafy path.

"Where's Sarah?" she asked, wondering belatedly if Sarah might not feel left out.

"She took the girls in to Bar Harbor for a junk food and trash culture run. Rock jewelry, stuff like that. Ice cream."

"*Sarah* took them in for that?"

They were climbing steadily now, up a steep, wooded slope. The path led through the trees in little switchbacks. The air smelled faintly of cinnamon.

"Sarah's not what you think, you know," Richie said, turning again to the trail. "I can see you thinking she's a purist about everything. I'm not sure you know what your sister's like. You have this idea that she's your mother; you keep trying to put your head in her lap. Didn't you ever think she might look up to you about some things?"

Laura laughed. "Right," she said; "she's jealous of my flawless management of my private life. Or is it my burgeoning career?"

Richie turned around and looked at her. "You really are a nitwit, aren't you," he said. Laura shook her head at him.

The last piece of climbing was up a stone staircase. The path had broadened, and a rail of fraying cedar steadied the angles.

"I think it's over here," said Richie, turning off to the right, and as he spoke Laura saw his head, which had been framed on the way up in the browns of the woods, suddenly surrounded by the aching blue sky. She felt the sun and ran a few steps to catch up. They walked up through abandoned terraces and gardens, to the summit.

The house had burned down years before. It had been made of stone, and could be seen from the islands for miles around. Where it had stood was now a great brick terrace, with a vast, windy view out across the smaller islands to the south. There were races that day, and the deep-blue channel below them was full of brilliant white sails, leaning steeply away from the wind.

When Richie sat down, Laura sat down beside him. The sun was hot on her face, after the climb, and they sheltered behind a stone bench, which kept the wind from them. She leaned back against it and closed her eyes. The only sound was the wind, a steady rush through the treetops.

"Well," said Richie. He had picked up some dry grass stems and was twisting them around each other. Laura looked at him, waiting. "What's going on?" he asked.

Laura bent her head. "I don't know what you mean."

"Are you all right? You seem very down."

Hearing Richie's gentle voice asking after her was almost too much for Laura. She turned her head away. "Oh, things will work out, I guess," she said into the wind.

"What?" Richie could not hear her.

"I said 'Things will work out,' " Laura said angrily.

"Hey," Richie said, putting his arm around her shoulders. "You look as though you're about to be shot." Laura tried to smile. "Tell me what's the matter."

Laura shrugged her shoulders and frowned. "Ward's mad at me for letting Nat come up here," she said.

Richie laughed. "So he should be. Wouldn't you be?"

"You're just like him."

Richie ignored this. He squeezed her shoulder again. "You're not listening. I said, wouldn't you be?" Laura said nothing, and he shook her.

Laura did not want to hear him. She pulled up a handful of the grass, and began, carefully, to shred it. Out in the deep water, the regatta had begun, and a dozen white sails, heeling heavily, were sliding across the blue channel. Against her will, Laura imagined herself returning to the house and finding Ward's ex-wife there. She picked at the grass. It was feathery and reddish.

"You think you're the only one who can get mad," said Richie. "You always think there's a good reason for you to get mad, but not for anyone else. If Ward gets mad, he's breaking the rules."

"He is," said Laura, like a child. She grinned at Richie.

"Yeah, right," said Richie. He smiled back at her. "Everybody does some things wrong every once in a while. You do yourself."

"No, I don't," said Laura, to make him laugh.

"Right," said Richie, "I forgot." He shook his head at her. "You're a bit of a spoiled brat, you know."

"I see," said Laura. She looked away from him down into the channel.

"What I mean is, you have your faults." Laura said nothing. She hated this whole conversation. "But, the thing is, most of us do." He looked at her. "Ward loves you anyway. In spite of your being a spoiled brat. You forget that. You think, if he's mad at me he doesn't love me. He could do both, you know." Laura frowned, watching the boats. The boats had their spinnakers set, in wild, lovely colors: raspberry, orange, great broad piratical stripes.

"We all love you anyway, in spite of any tiny faults. Don't you know that?" Laura still did not look at him. "We do. Sarah does. I do. I love you."

Laura put her head down. Her chest welled up without warning, and she felt her whole body break down. Richie pulled her toward him. "Hey," he said gently, and held her. Laura cried for a long time. It was what she longed for; something she was afraid was impossible. Hearing him say it was too much for her.

Laura's head was down on her crossed arms, which were propped on her knees. Between her feet the grass was green, the long shafts thick and sturdy, ending in feathery tips thick with seed. At the base of the stalks were dry, red brown shafts from last year. Insects moved jerkily among them. While Laura cried a small spotted spider crawled steadily up an angled stalk. She wondered what it would do when it got to the top, and found her tears slowing up.

Growing calmer, she raised her head and looked out again at the boats. She rubbed her wet face. The races were still going on, the sleek boats canted sideways on the dark water. She liked the look of their speed, their certainty, the practiced moves the crew would be making, knowing the gestures they must make, the words they must call out. Laura shook her hair away from her face and sat up straighter.

Richie smiled at her. "This is dumb," he said. Laura looked cautiously at him. "Really," he said. "Why are you so sad? Nat is eating his heart out for you, Ward is longing to marry you, Sammy dotes on you, we all love you, and you sit there in tears as though you don't have a friend in the world."

Laura began to laugh; she sniffed, rubbed her eyes and laughed again. "Yes, but you don't know about Ward. I don't think he's longing to marry me anymore. I mean, I think we're through. He sort of said so, last night." The words were terrible, by saying it she had made it real. Frightened, she wished she had not spoken.

"Did he say that?" Richie asked.

"He said he wasn't staying around for any more of this."

"Well, no, why should he?"

Laura looked at him, sniffed and laughed again.

"Well, okay," she said, "but if you really want to marry someone, you don't just clear off, the first mistake they make." She didn't say the rest: that she had known all along that Ward would leave once he knew what she was like.

"Dodo," Richie said, "everybody makes mistakes. It's what happens afterwards that makes the difference. Little tiny kids turn sulky and pissed off, and they say, You never loved me anyway. Grown-ups say they're sorry, and they try not to let it happen again."

Laura wouldn't look at him. He shook her, gently. She wouldn't turn. It was embarrassing to be shown to be so foolish. She picked a grass stem, and sucked thoughtfully at the fat, juicy end of it. Everything Richie was saying sounded right to her.

"You are so dumb," Richie said. "You don't think you can do anything."

"No," Laura said.

"But you can," Richie said. "There are things you can do besides sit around and feel sorry for yourself."

"Really?"

"For a start: have you apologized to Ward?"

"You are tough," Laura said.

"You are dumb," Richie said. Laura laughed.

When they got up, the afternoon was drawing in. The water below them was turning a deeper, murkier blue, and the wind was stronger. Only the racing boats were still out.

They found the trail at the edge of the woods, and started down the descent. The trees near the top were thin and scrubby, saplings, with an occasional wind-twisted pine. They walked on broad rocks, trimmed and laced with moss. The trail was marked with tiny cairns pointing the way. Richie stopped at a sharp switchback and stood back to let a lean, white-haired woman in blue sneakers and a windbreaker pass by. Behind her was a goofy golden retriever, his tail waving gently over his back.

"You haven't seen the warden, have you?" the woman asked gruffly.

"No," Richie said.

"I have to watch out for him. He's fined me twice for bringing the dog. The next time he sees me, he's going to take the dog."

"He won't take it away from you?" asked Laura.

The woman nodded. "He can," she said, "that's the rule." They all looked at the dog, who smiled vaguely, and shifted his tail at the attention. "I have to bring him," the woman said matter-of-factly; "he loves these walks."

Laura leaned over and patted the dog's broad head. He raised it to her hand and closed his eyes. Why did the woman bring him into these woods, she wondered; why risk it? But people chose their own risks, their own punishments.

They had come to the deep woods now, and, beside the path, lay fallen trees, big pine trunks covered with moss, slowly melting into the underbrush, the ferns curving harmoniously over their shapes. The rocks along the trail were cool and damp.

Laura wondered about Sarah. She had never imagined Sarah as seeing her as anything but a clumsy younger sister. She remembered the day Richie and Sarah had met; she remembered coming into the cool, shadowy hall at Inchfawn with Richie behind her.

Now she tried to imagine it from Sarah's point of view. What if she had stood, a newcomer in the big, dim house, and heard her sister come in, laughing and talking, with a strange young man? Seen the two of them cross the hall, loudly, easily, their bodies slick with sweat and ruddy with sun? Felt herself frozen and awkward, mute, at the top of the stairs? What if she had felt shy and excluded, hearing their voices; what if—looking down at her sister's long legs, long hair, short shorts—she had decided her own lengths were wrong, prim and dowdy?

The trail was easier now, the slope had gentled, and the trail itself was wider. Their strides had gotten longer, and Laura felt her limbs loosen in downhill rhythm.

And if Richie were right about Sarah, why was he not right about Ward? Certainly she should apologize, certainly she must make a move.

They came out on the gravel road that led back down to the parking lot. Below them was a pond, with a log cabin at the edge of it. Children were playing in the field, and shrieks came up to them on the wind.

Richie turned to her, smiling. He stretched and unrolled the sleeves of his red flannel shirt. He put his arm around her.

"All right?" he said.

"All right," Laura said, and smiled back.

Below them the children's cries rose and vanished on the wind. They were running across the field in patterns, like swallows wheeling in a pack. Behind them the pond shone in the lessening afternoon light, its iridescent glimmer restless against the calmer waves of grass.

Thirteen

When they got back, the house was quiet. Richie stretched, grinned and announced cheerfully that he was going to make himself a sandwich. Laura was not hungry, and went upstairs. She felt drained and empty—all that blowsy gush—and, after the sun and wind on the top of the hill, she wanted dark and quiet. Her pictures had been on her mind, and the solitude of the darkroom would be a relief. What Ward and Richie had told her was too threatening; she did not want to face it all directly.

She had turned a small, windowless dressing room on the second floor into a darkroom. Now she closed its door behind her and stood still in the darkness, breathing in the faint, sour, chemical smell. She moved across to the table and turned on the red safelight. Each object was neatly in place: the aluminum pans, the stacks of paper, the developing fluid, the cannisters—she knew their order and their functions. They were unchanged. She leaned over the small table, her hair swinging around her face, enclosing her field of vision: all she could see was the table with her tools, her objects, before her. The only motion, the only sounds, were those she made.

Laura took out two rolls of film from their cassettes and put them into the aluminum reels. She poured in the chemical developer and shook them gently back and forth. The films slid slowly against the sides, a quiet echo of her gestures. She wondered what Ward was doing: was he still angry? Was he playing tennis? Eating lunch? She saw him sitting with Allen Cartwright at the beach club, at one of the tables under the umbrellas. The wind was slapping at the waves in the sound beyond them—napkins, empty paper cups scattering across the ground. She saw Ward grin at Allen Cartwright, and, finished with his hamburger, crumple his napkin into a springy ball and throw it onto his paper plate. What did he think about, she wondered. The thought of his smile pained her, being no longer for her.

Laura took out the rolls from the chemical and hung them carefully on the line to dry. In the secret red of the safelight the long, dark strips glinted eerily, at once translucent and reflective. Now, alone in the dark, poised, waiting, she felt as though something was going to happen.

While the films were drying she set out the paper for the contact sheets, and then lay down idly on the narrow little bed, her chin propped up on the blanket at its foot. She remembered lying on Sarah's mahogany bed, the first time Sarah had come home from boarding school, a traveler from a strange land. Laura had lain there in silence, listening to stories of Sarah's new life, watching Sarah unpack her impossibly elegant school clothes: cable-knit wool socks that matched her sweaters, a Black Watch kilt in deep greens and blues; a gray blazer with navy piping; thick, rich sweaters. Laura was still in hand-me-downs, blue jeans and shapeless turtlenecks, cardigans dangerously thin at the elbow. Sarah stood over her suitcase, shaking out her good Fair Isle sweater, smoothing the sleeves down, then crossing them carefully over the breast. "I have two roommates," she told Laura. "One of them is Susan Goodhue. She's from Boston and has short, blond hair and is very nice. The other is Shou-Shou Chambers and she's from New York. She has long, dark hair and she's very pretty and very advanced." Sarah paused, holding up a skirt. She frowned at a spot on the skirt, held it up for examination: was it a spot? But it was only a wrinkle, and she put the skirt carefully on the skirt hanger, clamping it with just the right tension on the fabric. "She's kissed a boy," Sarah said, not looking at Laura. Laura rested her chin on the quilt, so that all of her face sank into the pale-lavender puff but her eyes. Sarah's roommate had kissed a boy. She might as well have been making grenades: how had she dared? And her sister, how could Sarah dare to enter this rapid, hurtling stream of events; how could she have plunged into it? She, Laura, would never dare it. Sarah hung the skirt neatly in the closet, and turned again to her suitcase. She did not look at Laura. Now, lying on the bed in her darkroom, Laura could see that Sarah herself had been frightened by her roommate.

When the films were dry, she took them carefully off the line, holding them by the edges so there would be no finger marks. She slid them into the contact printer. This, now, was what she loved. She pressed down on the glass and turned on the enlarging light. It was this moment, the moment waiting for the images to appear. Laura's heart rose in her chest; there was always, each time, the hope, the lovely wild possibility of something perfect arising to her eyes, something that would hold her in perfect suspension, something that would utterly ravish.

The enlarging light was brilliant in the darkroom. Laura bent over the paper, waiting. This was the last of the tree series. The first groups she had done were the high branching shapes, the brushy tops against the sky, arching in the wind, still against the clouds. Next she had done the shapes of trees against one another, the patterns of the forest. These last ones, this series, would be the end: they were close-ups of the bark, of the delicate filigrees of the tree itself.

As the darkening patches appeared in patterns on the paper, as images were slowly formed, coalescing in a magical union of light and liquid, they created shapes: not hers. Laura bent over them, frowning. She could not make them out. She felt the same anxious dislocation that she had when Ward and Richie had talked to her. Slowly, she could see that the shapes, instead of the careful precision of bark patterns, instead of the abstract forms of tree trunks and limbs, were resolving themselves into human limbs. Arms and legs, and she remembered. She had taken a picture of Pia lying in the hammock from directly overhead. Laura had stood on a rickety wicker rocker, and Pia's face beneath her was smooth and pale, the round eyes staring directly up at heaven. It was not a tree. Laura looked at the rest of them: it was a roll of pictures she had forgotten about, shots of people around the house. Expecting trees, Laura found the faces, the arms and legs had a strangeness to them, an unfamiliar aspect. Pia looked remote and unflawed, a child-Madonna with an ancient face, and an air of inward reflection. It drew Laura's interest. Was this what Pia was really like? Quiet, solitary, Pia watched her flamboyant older sister, and led her own life. She read in the hammock for hours at a time. What did she read? Laura wondered; what was she like? Laura hovered over the tiny square, squinting.

When the sheet was ready, Laura turned off the enlarging light and took the contact sheet out to look at it with a magnifier. Next to Pia was Karin, a close-up. The girl was shown in profile, learning forward, her eyebrows raised, her mouth open. She was talking energetically. She could have been twenty. She was at that elastic stage when the features are mature and the skin is not lined; she could have been anywhere between fifteen and twenty-five. Her energy was visible: she was probably talking about parents, or eating habits, or the general hatefulness of the world in which she found herself. Laura shook her head, irritated. But she paused, caught, by the innocence of Karin's raised eyebrows. What else should she be thinking about, at fifteen? Laura felt something loosen inside her, relax. Poor Karin, she thought, always enraged: what has taught her that life must be attacked, the world must be held at bay? It's what I do, Laura thought painfully. I do that. With the sheet in her hand Laura sat down on the bed. The room was dim around her. Ward, she thought anxiously. Ward, Ward. She put the contact sheet down. This was how she was with Ward: furious, defensive, stubborn, ungenerous—why did he put up with it? What was it she expected from him? The small bed creaked as she shifted her weight. It was metal, painted white, with brass knobs at each corner. It seemed impossibly narrow now, but she had slept on a bed that size for years after she had reached her grown-up size. Imagine the cramp; imagine the terrible silence, the great lack of sleeping alone, she thought, the exhaustion of knowing that beyond your leg lay nothing, no other body, no other warmth. Yet still it seemed so dangerous to Laura, this close involvement: what did people want? What were they up to? She thought of Richie on the hillside: "We all love you," he had said. She shook her head. Would that be true? What if that were true? It was a dazzling thought, frightening.

Next to Karin was a picture of Sarah. She looked terrible. Her chin was tucked in, creasing itself into deep folds. She was talking, and her mouth was pursed and tense. Behind her on the wall was a marine print: Laura remembered the scene. They had been in the living room one evening, and Sarah had been arguing with Richie.

And what did that all mean? Laura wondered. Why were all these rough edges so apparent? What about all those unkind responses, sharp replies? Was theirs a good marriage? Was Sarah going to get divorced? She had always believed

Sarah knew how to be married properly. But then was this the way a proper marriage went along, halting and spitting, jerking and sputtering?

The next picture was Ward, very close up, from the front. She held the magnifier over it. Seen from the side, Ward had an Etruscan profile, the long, straight nose, the large, wide-set eyes, the loose mane of hair. Seen from the front he looked less noble: you could see that his mouth was slightly crooked, and his cheeks were full. He was looking directly at Laura, and, faced with his direct, brown gaze, she felt abashed.

Laura bent down to examine his face, his eyes. She did not know, really, what had happened the night before. What did it all amount to? It should somehow have been final: she had hit Ward in the face, and he her. These were unforgivable acts, were they not? That should be that, then? She put the sheet down. If she were going to be honest, she would have to admit that she had goaded Ward into hitting her. She had started the fight: why had she done that? Thinking now of his leg thrown over hers in bed, remembering his hand smoothing back her hair, she could not imagine why she had done it. But if she were, still, going to be honest, she would have to admit there were times when she felt safer when Ward was angry with her. Then she knew where she was. Laura stared soberly into the glowing darkness.

What Ward had said was true: I must change, she thought, and felt at once brave and frightened. She hoped it was not too late.

The second contact sheet was trees, as planned. The images were what Laura had wanted: sober attention to detail on Nature's part. The patterns on the bark were far too regular for chance. They looked, like hieroglyphics, as though they would yield to the patient scholar some ancient knowledge, some long and vital story. These were what Laura was after:

signs, forms, shapes she could control. She would print them later in the week. Waiting for that, knowing of the pictures, would be a pleasure. They were a secret wealth in her mind.

What Richie had said had begun to seep into her, raising up Laura's heart. If it were true, then things were different after all. It went against all her assumptions, a strange, leavening notion of salvation.

"Richie loves me," Laura said out loud, and the words, in the dim, red light, the small, dark room, seemed rich and magical, an incantation. Everything might be different. Laura said it again. Saying the words, she felt swollen, frightened, strengthened.

Down in the kitchen she got out the plate of cold lamb and began to cut it up for curry. She wondered where Nat and Sammy were. She should have found out when Nat's plane was and ordered him a taxi, otherwise he'd end up spending another night. Laura cut at the pinky-brown wedges of meat. She would be very firm with Nat. She would not get angry. She would simply make it clear that he could not stay. There were women who could say that sort of thing. He could go to a motel. Why not? There was the Asticou, right at the head of the harbor, and there was The Ledges, or whatever it was called. Laura finished with the lamb, and swept it with her hands into a damp, cool heap. She picked up an onion and took off the papery, crackling outer skin of it, which crumbled in her hand. Underneath was the firm crisp whiteness, and she took off the thick outer layer, revealing the glistening, iridescent, transparent one beneath.

Laura heard footsteps and looked up. Sammy and Nat appeared from the beach. They were wrinkled, sandy and sunburned. Sammy's eyelids were heavy; she could see he was exhausted. Nat, behind him, gave her an uncertain smile. He patted Sammy on the shoulder, as though to remind her of his position in the household. Sammy leaned heavily against him. Laura saw they had the same bold eyebrows, the same pouty lower lip, and that on the beach they had done something together, knitted into each other, formed something. There was something between them.

"Hello," Laura said, "did you have a nice time?"

Sammy came over to her and laid his head against her leg. "We built a sand castle," he said.

Laura smiled at Nat. "Good. Listen, before I forget it, tell me what time your plane leaves and we'll call you a taxi."

"Oh," said Nat, smoothing his hair back from his forehead. "The flight tonight was full. I'm on the six-eighteen tomorrow morning, if that's okay." He was tentative, uneasy, and it made him sound breezy and arrogant.

Angry, Laura turned back to the onions. They lay gleaming before her, peeled, pale and glistening. She began to slice them, feeling them yield, crisp and moist. She said nothing.

"I guess I should have told you before," Nat said. "I *know* I should have asked you before. I just forgot."

Laura did not look up. Now what should she do? She could feel Nat's uncertainty. Of course he hadn't told her before, because he was afraid of being turned out. But really, she thought, how exasperating of him. Still, I can't tell him to leave. I am not one of those women who can say No, simply No.

Nat spoke to Sammy. "Uh-oh," he said. "Looks like I'll have to head on out, Sambo. Looks like your mom doesn't want me here. Sleep in the car somewhere. Poor Daddy."

Sam moved to the table and sat down on a chair. He rubbed a finger along the oilcloth.

"Don't you do that," Laura said angrily to Nat. "Don't you do that to Sammy." Nat shrugged his shoulders, pretending innocence. Laura turned to Sammy. "Your daddy can spend tonight here, Sambo. But it's kind of rude, you know, to *tell* someone that you're spending the night with them, not wait to be asked. You know that." Laura finished with the onions and swept them into a shimmery, pungent heap. Sammy stared at the tablecloth, and Nat said nothing. He shifted his weight to the other hip, his arms crossed over his chest. Karin came in the door and Nat turned, pleased at the interruption.

"Ah, Veg-a-rama," he said.

Laura expected Karin to turn rude and sulky, but instead she giggled, tossing her long hair. She was wearing a red tank suit and brown corduroy pants, and, beneath the thin, shiny fabric, her nipples stood out clearly in gentle points.

"Oh," she said, "it's the Animal Murderer."

Sammy moved back to Laura and again leaned against her leg. He spoke into her skin, his breath warm and damp against her, like a calf's.

"Karin helped us build the sand castle."

"And Pia?" Laura asked. Nat stood before Karin, all angles, his arms tight across his chest, his chin tilted up, his back arched: look at me, his angles said, take me seriously.

"Only Karin," Sammy murmured. "She doesn't like to be tickled, either." Laura saw the two of them on the beach, Karin's struggle in Nat's arms, the abandon of the surroundings, the casual sand, the lapping water.

Laura put oil and butter into the skillet and turned on the heat beneath it. She watched the butter dissolve into a transparent pool. She put in the onions and stirred them.

"I bet you wouldn't," Karin was saying to Nat. "You wouldn't, would you?"

"Nat," said Laura firmly, her back to him, "if you're going to spend the night, I'd like you to pitch in a bit. Would you please take Sammy upstairs and give him a bath? Or a shower with you if you'd rather. And Karin, would you please set the table? We're seven; I'll give Sammy a yogurt and put him to bed."

Nat clapped his heels together and saluted, stiff-legged and deep-chinned. "Aye, aye," he said. "Come on, Sam."

Karin moved easily around the kitchen, lithe and supple. Laura watched her carrying the stack of plates into the dining room, the heavy dishes balanced against her narrow midriff, the slippery fabric sliding against her skin. *"Don't stand, don't stand so, don't stand so close to me,"* she sang, over and over, in a queer monotonous, rhythm. Laura wondered what sort of social life she had at home. Were there rules, restrictions? Or were teenagers now too powerful for them? It would be like living with a time bomb, Laura thought, one that would go off again and again.

The onions began to cook, sweet, hot, translucent in the dark pan. Why was it so pleasant to stand before the stove, smelling the butter, vaguely stirring at the trailing semicircles of onion, building the idea of the dinner that she would present to everyone? She was very good at curry. She made a terrific curry.

While the rice was cooking and the curry simmering Laura went upstairs to change for dinner. She wondered if Ward was home. She must be the one to do something first, she thought; she had started the fight. Still, she was frightened.

When she opened the bedroom door, she found Ward standing in the middle of the rug. He was fresh from the shower and naked except for a damp towel wrapped around his waist. It came down to his ankles, a thick, damp, blue toga. He looked lordly in it, his big, burly chest springing out from the cloth, his curly, blond hair a fine dense mist across the center.

"Hi," he said affably.

Laura shut the door behind her. "I'm sorry about last night," she said. "I was awful."

But Ward was not to be won. "Thank you," he said, kind but distant. "What's on for tonight?"

"Curry for dinner," Laura said, "and Nat says he couldn't get on the flight tonight. He's leaving first thing in the morning." She waited.

Ward nodded, looking into space. "Great," he said absently, then turned to Laura. "Really great."

"I'm sorry—"

"No, no," said Ward, holding up his hand. "Old Asshole's got a fine ear for nuance, doesn't he? Knows just when he's wanted."

"Ward," said Laura, "I'm sorry this happened. All of it. It's my fault and I apologize. Do you want me to go downstairs and tell him to get his suitcase and go to a motel? I'll tell him that if you want." She put her hand on the doorknob. "Do you want me to?"

Ward waved his hand and shook his head. "Don't bother," he said. He walked back to the bathroom, the towel hanging in heavy folds around his legs. He took it off and tossed it easily onto the bathroom floor. He stood still for a moment, rubbing his chest thoughtfully, moving his hand through the soft tangle of hair, his fingers firm and authoritative and absentminded on his own flesh. Laura watched him. He turned around to her.

"Oh, no," he said affably, and waved his hand. "No, I think this will be swell. We didn't have quite enough action last night: I can see why you'd want to go on. You've got a real nose for dramatic interest; I think you should give up on still photography and become a theatrical director. Ingmar Bergman move over. This girl's got the nose." With a grand gesture Ward touched his own, bold Roman nose, and Laura giggled.

"Ward," she said, "what do you want from me? Tell me what you want me to do and I'll do it."

Ward scratched his neck, starting with the base of it, where the collarbones met, moving up its length to the jut of his chin. "Nothing," he said mildly. "I like your plan. Theater as therapy, every evening a new showcase of talent."

Laura sat down on the bed. She could not tell his mood. What did he mean by this offhand distancing? It kept her from throwing herself at him, drained her of her determination.

"Well, it's the last time it will happen. I want you to know that," she said. "I'm going to put Sammy to bed early."

"I wish you'd put me to bed early."

"I will if you want," Laura said, but Ward did not answer. "I'm going to put Sammy to bed and give him some yogurt and take a shower, and I'll meet you downstairs."

Ward bowed, naked. "You will indeed," he said. "I'll meet you *and* your husband downstairs."

When she came back down from Sammy's room, Ward had gone.

Karin appeared at the dinner table looking flushed and shining. She had washed her hair, and she wore a silky shirt that kept sliding off her shoulders, and no bra. She sat next to Nat and kept tossing her head to keep her slippery blond hair out of her eyes. She gleamed like a pearl. Again and again she tossed her hair out of her eyes. She could not keep from smiling, obscurely excited, feeling something new, feeling part of a current that touched her, touched an edge of her, that threatened to flood through her. Bored, sullen, restless, she had been waiting for this current. Karin wanted more than anything to be awakened, to be swept into something besides the life she saw stretching out before her forever, the tedious slavery of her parents, the killing monotony of school. Unwitting, she waited for something to rouse her. So she laughed, giddy, and flung her hair back out of her eyes, and let her silky shirt fall again and again off her smooth shoulder.

The curry was good, smooth and spicy and rich. Laura watched Ward, as he started eating his, but he did not look at her.

"So," said Ward to Sarah, "how was Bar Harbor?"

"Did you see my church?" asked Richie.

"I did not see your church," Sarah said, shaking her head and smiling.

"There's a church in Bar Harbor," Richie explained. "I've seen photographs of it. It's small. American gothic at its peak. It's got wooden tracery along the roofline that looks like lace. I've never been able to find it. Every time I go there, I have the feeling that it's moving, that it's just around the corner, on the next block. And I think I did see it, once. I think I saw it the summer I lived up here with my aunt, but I can't quite remember if I really did or if I'm imagining it from the photograph. It drives me crazy." Richie pressed his fists against his temples and squinted, gritting his teeth. "Will I ever find it?"

"Ah," said Ward, "the bluebird of Bar Harbor?"

"Maeterlinck was nuts, you know," announced Laura, desperately trying to win Ward's attention. "He spent the last years of his life trying to prove that someone's horse could count, and talk Greek."

"Sounds like Virginia Woolf," said Sarah, "but with her it was pigeons."

Nat was talking to Karin. "You have a rash," he said. "You have spots all over your face," he said. Karin was flushed with sun, her pale, milky skin was spread with a rosy glow from her afternoon on the beach. Freckles had begun to appear on her face and across her shoulders.

"Those are freckles," Karin said tossing her hair.

"Those are spots," Nat said. "They're a very serious symptom of meat deficiency. Only vegetarians get them, look at Pia." Pia had spent the afternoon reading in the hammock, and her skin was pale and untouched.

"They are freckles," Karin insisted, "from the sun."

"They're really bad," said Nat. "Go into any health food store and you'll see people covered with them. You have them all over. Look, here, and here."

Nat put his hand on Karin's shoulder. Her shirt slid off it, and Laura saw that Karin's flesh, beneath Nat's hand, rose up to meet him instead of twisting away. Only for an instant.

She ducked her head and pulled her shoulder out of his touch gracefully, pulling up her shirt again.

"You have them all over," Nat said again, pleased. He picked up his wine glass.

"Now, Karin," Ward said, "tell me everything you did in Bar Harbor. What do you think of it? Is it your favorite place in the world? Is it a hopeless hick town? What are the people like? We count on you for the youth view."

Karin composed herself, pushing again at her shirt and narrowing her eyes.

"First we went to the rock shop, because Mom likes all those colored rock jewelry things."

"Do you like them?" asked Laura.

"No," Karin said. "They're just rocks."

"You don't like them? I'd have thought they'd be just your style," Ward said. "Egalitarian, all that."

"Yeah, but, see, they're ugly," Karin said patiently.

"A new angle," said Ward. "The role of esthetics in political theory. A great subject for a thesis."

"I," said Karin boldly, "am not going to college."

Laura noticed that Nat had poured her some wine.

"Good," said Ward, nodding. "You'll save your father and mother about fifty thousand dollars." He grinned at Richie. "You're rich." Richie groaned.

"My father," said Karin, "already knows it." She liked center stage; she liked sitting at the table with the candlelight flickering over her face, the red wine in the glass before her, grown-ups listening to what she said. "I've planned my life out exactly." There was a pause.

"Well?" Nat said. "Let's see. You're going to be the first woman to win the poker championship. No-Limit Hold 'Em at Las Vegas." Karin gave him an elaborate look of disgust, rolling her eyes up in her head.

"You're going to be a stewardess on the first space shuttle," Richie said.

"A stewardess," Karin said witheringly.

"Now, Richie," said Sarah, protectively. She smiled at Karin. "Let's see. Are you going to run an ashram?"

"Ma," Karin complained, "you guys are all so out of it. I'm going to be a midwife."

"A midwife!" Nat pounced. "Just vegetarian births?"

"I think you'd make a very good midwife," Sarah said.

Ward smiled at Karin. "I do too," he said, and the way he smiled at Karin, relaxed, warm, attentive, made Laura feel suddenly apprehensive. A clamor started inside her. She was *not,* she told herself, jealous of a fifteen-year-old. But she wished Ward would look at her—Laura. Karin's shoulder was again bare, and now Nat was leaning forward, talking to her, making her laugh again, and she was sweeping the silky hair back from her face. Laura wondered if Nat could see down the front of Karin's loose blouse. If he could, would he?

"Nat," she said, "I forgot to give you the name of the driver. The taxi for tomorrow."

"Oh, right, right," Nat said, nodding, vague.

"You'd better call right now," Laura said firmly. "There's only one man who drives, it's not like New York."

"Right," said Nat, but he did not move until Laura pushed her chair back and stood over him.

Then he stood at once, polite, neat, his collar in trim points over his sweater. Laura remembered the fuss he made about clothes: "Does this look right?" he would say, turning his head back and forth in the mirror, trying to catch his profile unawares. "That looks fine," Laura would say mildly: what else could she say? But she hated his vanity, his preening.

The telephone was in an alcove in the hall leading to the stairs. A rickety wicker table, with a faded cloth that hung in deep folds to the floor, held the telephone and an old lamp. This had a yellowed, ancient shade, and gave out a rich, intense light that shone on the table alone. The rest of the tiny alcove was dense with shadows. Laura bent over the table to find the taxi number. She could feel Nat standing behind her. She knew exactly how he stood, she could feel where he put his weight. She turned and looked at him, and he, unprepared, smiled uncertainly at her.

The obedient sweetness of it undid Laura. "Oh, Nat," she said, meaning that she was sorry about everything: how she had not helped him or given him a chance; how, now, she wished him to be happy; how the sadness of things rose up—the moth that fluttered up from the table, the dim light, the cluttered table—all of it part of the current of sadness that ran through things. Laura thought for a moment of holding him, as though by sheer physical intensity she could for a moment stop the current, the two of them, for an instant, out of its coldness.

It would not be fair to ask if he forgave her.

"I'm sorry," she said, anyway. He smiled at her, kindly, and shook his head.

"It's over," he said gently.

Laura had never seen Nat like this, never seen him grave and sensible. She felt faintly cheated: it seemed to be Nat who was moving ahead into a larger world, and she who was unable to take the leap.

The two of them faced each other in the glow of the yellow lamp. The room was tiny, the roof barely inches above their heads. The space enclosed them, set them off from the world. All Laura had to do was slightly shift her stance, alter faintly the way she stood, lean into him, and the flow between them would change. She remembered loving him, and she would have liked to give him something besides his misery.

But things had shifted around them; he was right. She moved gently away, smiling. Karin appeared in the doorway.

"Oh, *hi,*" she said, elaborately, surprise drenching her face. "I thought you'd gone out or something."

"You'd better call now," Laura said. "I've written the number down for you." She smiled at Karin, stepping past her in the narrow hallway. Karin stood indecisively in the thick yellow light, next to Nat.

Fourteen

A dim light came in from the kitchen, but at the table the only illumination was from the full glow of the candles. Only the fronts of the faces were lit, as though only that side, for that moment, was public, and the rest of each person was shrouded and secret. In the center of the table was a jug filled with flowers—devil's paintbrush, daisies and sweet pink clover, their colors muted in the candlelight. The remains of the curry lay in rich mustardy swags on the white plates, and the wine was a deep, ruby gleam in the heavy cut-glass goblets. Beyond the table were the big windows, to the floor, and beyond the windows was the dense blue black of the sky, the trees, and beyond, the harbor.

Sarah was smoothing her napkin, neatly folded, over and over, her narrow finger running up and down the white square. Richie was watching her.

"Sarah," he said, as though he were giving a warning signal. She did not look up.

Laura pulled her chair out and sat down. Sarah turned to her.

"I do think it's *strange,*" she said, her words very precise. "I think it's *strange* that Nat would act that way with a fifteen-year-old girl, in front of her parents, don't you?" There was a pause. Sarah looked at Richie. "Don't you think it's strange?" Sarah spoke as though this were a purely intellectual problem, having nothing to do with Karin's bare shoulder, her silky hair, Nat's strange, older hand on Karin's skin. Sarah's life seemed suddenly visible to Laura, painful, full of rage denied. Laura could see how tightly bound her sister was; it was a terrible vision. She put her hand on Sarah's shoulder, but Sarah looked at her blankly. She would take nothing from her younger sister.

"Hey," Richie said, leaning across the table to his wife. He put out his hand and took Sarah's wrist. "Babe," he said, and Sarah's eyes flicked to him. Richie shook his head at her. "You're making much too much of this," he said, worrying at her wrist, shaking it a bit. "Trust me." He smiled at her. "It's play," he said, "it's just play."

"Nat's just being a jerk," Laura offered disloyally. "He's trying to establish himself as a male in this household, that's all."

"The guy's just an—" Ward began, but Laura cut in.

"Richie's right, he's just playing. It doesn't mean anything. Anyway, let's stop it. Let's all do something together. Let's play a game."

"Let's play The Game," said Richie.

Laura went upstairs to check on Sammy. She didn't want to be associated with playing The Game. Ward didn't like it, and, at the moment, she wasn't sure that he liked her. When she came down, the teams were chosen: Richie, Karin, Laura and Pia were on one side; Nat, Sarah and Ward on the other. How, she wondered, had Nat and Ward ended up on the same team? They stood now at the sink, Ward rinsing, Nat putting things in the dishwasher. Ward stood solidly on his heels, his shoulders back, his head high. He moved slowly, rather majestically. He didn't turn when Laura came in. Nat stood uneasily on his toes, his shoulders curved protectively around his chest. Between plates, Nat touched his hair, stroked his nose, tucked his shirt in tighter to his pants. He saw Laura and grinned, holding up a plate.

"You didn't think I knew about all this, did you?"

"You never let on," Laura said. "First you're reading books, now you're doing dishes. A real paragon. Some nice girl will snap you up in no time."

"I'm highly versatile," he said, his mouth turning self-conscious and tense. "I'm great in the kitchen. I'm also turning out to be great with a gun. I've been practicing at a shooting gallery out in New Jersey." He looked around. Ward was working on a pot. Laura was putting the curry away. "I've really gotten quite good at it," he said hopefully, but no one responded.

"That it?" Ward asked Laura, looking around the room, not at her.

"I think so," she said. They spoke as though Nat and his wistful remarks about pistols were not with them, as though they were alone in the old kitchen at night. Laura wished they were: alone in the whole house, and friends. Ward dried his hands off with finality. "The Game," he said, turning around and looking at Laura, at Sarah and Richie and the girls, as though he had just turned Nat off like a light. Laura wondered if it would help if she went up to bed. But the point was to try to cheer Sarah up, everyone playing together. Then what was she to do about Ward? He had not really spoken to her all evening.

Laura's team got the living room; the others went into the extra parlor to think up their entries. Outside, the damp was rising off the harbor in shifting layers of white. They lit the fire, and Laura sank into the deep cushions on the sofa. For dinner she had changed into a long, purple dress of cotton jersey, with a red sash around her hips. Her hair hung halfway down her back, and she looked—in flickering firelight, one bare foot framed by the purple fabric—like a stage gypsy, dressed for *Carmen.*

"Othello," she offered Richie.

Richie nodded. "Not bad," he said, "but one-word ones are too easy."

"How would you do it?" asked Laura, nettled. She thought of herself, really, as being an authority on playing The Game.

"Just pick up a handkerchief and carry on," said Richie. He was stretched out in a beaten-down armchair, his long legs stretched in front of him. The sleeves of his sweater pushed up, his glasses down on his nose, the paper and pencil before him made him look academic, a graduate student at work on his thesis. Laura could feel him settling into this; he was serious.

"Well, why can't we give it to Sarah? Nat wouldn't know Othello from Superman," Laura said scornfully. Karin looked at her.

"Let's give Nat 'The B-52's,' she said challengingly. "The rock group," she added, for the ignorant.

Laura smiled at her: how glamorous Nat must seem to her, she thought. "That's good, but two people on the team have to know it."

"What about *Casablanca?"* Pia asked.

"Actually, that's a good one," Laura said.

"Easy," Richie pronounced. "Forty-five seconds."

"How would you do it?" Laura asked.

"Be Bogart. Pull your trenchcoat around you, pull your hat down over your eyes, light a cigarette. A piece of cake."

"Oh, all right," said Laura, smiling at Pia. "Then *you* think of some," she told Richie.

"Anna Karenina," Richie said.

"Pooh," Laura said, showing off. "Thirty seconds."

"What?" Richie looked up from his strips of paper. "You tell me how."

On the mantelpiece stood a row of copper luster jugs. The firelight, rising and falling, brought out intermittent flickers in their brown depths. Below them sat the two girls, on a bench before the fire. On the low seat they looked the same size, the same age, their long legs stretched out before them, their blond hair in swags about their shoulders. They leaned forward, watching their father and aunt compete with each other. No matter how they looked, Laura thought, they would not be thinking the same things: Karin was in racing gear, waiting for Nat to reappear, critical of Laura, she imagined. She wondered if Pia knew how Karin felt, or if that heated wave of unchildlike emotion swirled out to him unnoticed, like a sound too high for her to hear.

Ward pounded on the wall from the other room. "Are you ready? We're coming, ready or not."

Under pressure, Richie wrote down a string of titles—too easy, too obscure, too well-known—none of them quite right, but the others were drifting in, standing impatiently at the living room door.

"Okay," Ward said. He took off his watch and handed it to Laura. "One of us has to go twice, so you give us one first." Laura gave him his slip: *A Cruising Guide to the New England Coast.* She smiled up at him as she handed it over; Ward studied it, his head tilted to one side, one hand in the pocket of his corduroys.

"Hmm," he said, without looking at Laura. "Get out the alternate list," he said to Sarah. "Switch to Plan B." He was cross.

Ward put the slip in his pocket and began, making the briefest-possible eye contact with Laura for her to start the stopwatch on him. He held out his hands, flat, side by side and open like a book, to signal what sort of title he'd been given; next he held up eight fingers for the number of words in it. He held up one finger—first word—then made a long "C" with his thumb and forefinger, the symbol for "little word." "A . . . An . . . The" his team shouted at once, and Ward clapped his hands and pointed at Sarah, who had offered the "A." Now he got down to it: he held up two fingers for "second word," then he put the fingers on his forearm, to show number of syllables. He was trying to act out *Cruising:* he was a glider, lilting through the clouds, his arms stiffly out at shoulder level, his face rigid. Laura began to laugh. She moved over and sat next to the two girls on the low bench, aligning herself with immaturity and hilarity.

"Hang glider," said Nat.

"Butterfly," said Sarah.

"Lunatic," said Laura, and the girls began to giggle.

They could not get it, though Ward soared and lifted, getting angrier and angrier. At last he gave up, and switched to a brisk demonstration of sailing—hauling on lines, pushing tillers about, watching the sail.

"Ready about!" called Sarah.

"Hard a' lee," said Pia, having just learned this.

"Come about," guessed Sarah.

"Come together," said Nat unhelpfully.

Sarah was sitting on the edge of her chair, her feet pressed neatly together, her hand a tight fist under her chin. She made careful, infrequent guesses. Nat sat next to her, his knees apart, his shirt rumpled. He ran his hand through his hair constantly, and made absurd guesses. What he liked was the shouting.

When the three minutes were up, Ward stood up straight again, regaining his dignity, and read out the title.

"Oh, no," said Nat loudly, "not fair. Out of the question. No one in the world has heard of it."

"As a matter of fact a great many people have heard of it," Laura said at once, "including both of your teammates."

Nat turned to Sarah. "Sarah? Have you been reading that trash?"

Sarah confessed. "I'm afraid I have heard of it."

Nat held his hands up in the air as though Laura held a gun. "Par-*don,*" he said, using the French pronunciation.

"It's a perfectly legitimate title," Laura said.

"Let's give Laura the whopper," Ward said.

Sarah handed her the slip. Laura took it, her heart pounding, anxious over Ward, excited by the game. She looked at the title: "Ozymandias." Pia and Karin would never have heard of it. Richie might—but what if he didn't? She waved the slip of paper at Ward, and said warningly, "Someone on my team has to know this besides me."

Ward waved his hand. "Our sources assure us."

Laura looked again at the paper. The first syllable rhymed with nothing; she would have to act "Oz" itself. The wizard in his balloon? Dorothy and Toto? The Cowardly Lion biting his tail and roaring? Pia and Karin should get that. Staring at the paper, she felt a sudden wash of fear: what if Ward had decided to leave? What if it were too late? She looked up at her team. Richie had moved down with the girls, and the three of them leaned forward, their elbows on their knees, their faces eager. Laura looked at Ward. He and Sarah and Nat sat in an awkward row on the sofa. Ward's mouth was set in an unfriendly line; Sarah had crossed her legs and her arms, as if to keep as much as possible as far away as possible. Nat looked casual and out of place, beside them.

"Ready?" Ward asked sternly.

Laura nodded. Her heart felt frantic. She put the paper down on the table and took a deep breath.

"Go," said Ward.

She scribbled quickly in the air.

"Poem," Richie said.

She held up one finger, for one word, then spread five fingers on her forearm to show syllables. She held up one finger to show first syllable. With billowing gestures she sketched a flowing mane around her head, then placed a crown on it. Turning wild, she gave a ferocious, soundless roar.

"King Kong," said Richie.

Laura ignored him. She looped a long tail over her arm, looked fearful, gave a timid little leap and bit the end of her tail.

"Dairy Queen," Nat suggested. Karin giggled.

Laura roared again, whimpered, bit her tail. It was Pia who got it: "The Cowardly Lion," she said. Laura pointed at Pia, clapped, then begged with her hands, wheedling for another thought on the same subject, another interpretation, more offerings.

"Dorothy," said Karin.

"The Wizard," said Richie.

"Sergeant Yukon," Nat put in, lunatic.

Laura shook her head, still pleading, still beckoning with her hands.

"Toto?" guessed Pia.

"Tonto," said Nat, but at the same time Karin said "The Wizard of Oz," and Laura clapped her hands in celebration. The next syllable, "see," was simple—she pointed at her eyes, at a lamp, and Richie shouted out " 'Oz-see-mandias'!" They all cheered: it had taken forty-eight seconds.

Laura's team won both rounds. Pia and Karin turned out to be demon guessers, beating their hands on their knees, infected by Laura and Richie's manic energy. They called out words, names, quotes at random. Richie leaned forward, cheering and clapping. When they got a title, they shouted and hugged each other. The other team turned more and more somber, except for Nat, who had brought up the wine bottle, and who made more and more extraordinary guesses, primarily for entertainment.

At the end of the second round, Nat got up and stretched, and said he had to get up early the next morning for his plane.

Everyone moved a bit, shifting limbs, stretching, preparing to abandon the evening.

"Well, you guys were fabulous," Laura said to Pia and Karin.

"That was fun," Karin said cheerfully.

At least the flirtation had been broken up, Laura thought. She looked at Sarah's sober face, her tightly closed arms. She wished Sarah would relax. She wished, while she was at it, that Ward would stop being mad at her.

Nat went around the room saying goodbye.

"Goodbye, you two," he said, leaning down and kissing the girls awkwardly. "I hope you work things out someday. Don't kill each other."

"Can't promise," Karin said at once, and Pia pushed her without rancor.

Nat kissed Sarah, shook hands with Richie, and turned finally to Ward, putting out his hand theatrically.

"Goodbye, Ward," he said. "Thanks for putting me up. Thanks for putting up with me." He laughed self-consciously.

"Not at all," Ward said, his eyes opaque.

"Are we on the same flight again tomorrow?"

"Not this time, I'm afraid. I'm staying up for a while." Laura's heart lifted at that.

"Ah." Nat turned to Laura, putting out his hand, and unexpectedly she leaned forward and gave him a kiss. Poor Nat, she thought, he hasn't had an easy time of it. But the kiss embarrassed her as soon as she had done it, and she lunged backward, stumbling over the rug. She could then think of nothing to say, conscious of Ward's unfriendly eyes.

"Goodbye," she said, backing off.

"Goodbye," Nat said, "thanks for having me. I really"—he paused, looking around—"enjoyed myself." It was so obviously false that everyone laughed, including Nat. He shrugged his shoulders, gave a little sort of salute to them all and went upstairs. As Sarah turned, Laura caught her by the shoulders and hugged her.

"I love you," she whispered to her sister. "Don't worry."

Sarah turned, round-eyed. "About what?"

"Anything," Laura said firmly. That was all you could do, she thought, send out the message.

Fearful at facing Ward, Laura stayed down alone to put the room back in order, when the others had gone upstairs. The room looked, with the dying fire, the deeply rumpled pillows, abandoned but replete. Something had filled the space, the core of it. Above the mantelpiece was a print of a clipper ship coming into a harbor. The name of the ship—*Intrepid*—was written below it in a flowing, painstaking script. The sails were bellied out clean and precise, and the waves were small and helpful. It was an ideal of order. Punching up the pillows, straightening the tables, smoothing out the little woven rug that lay in the middle of the bigger gray one, Laura restored the room to correspond with the calm precision of the picture. Looking around the room, she felt sure and effective. The room looked as she wanted it. She turned out the light and went upstairs to Ward.

He was already in bed, and headed for solitary sleep: the light on his side turned out. Laura shut the door behind her softly and began to undress, her movements gentle.

"I hope you didn't mind that too much," she said, tentatively. "I think it helped Sarah. I mean, it pulled the evening together."

"I know *you* love playing it," Ward said. He sat up angrily.

"I do like it," admitted Laura.

"You're very unpleasant to play with, do you know that?"

Laura sat down on the bed. "Well, I don't mean to be, and I'm sorry you think so."

"God!" said Ward, throwing himself back against the pillow. "You make it into the goddamned Olympics. It's just supposed to be fun; it's not supposed to be an international competition."

"I do get excited," Laura said mildly, "but I don't think I'm as bad as you say I am." It was a relief to see Ward so angry over something so trivial.

"You get absolutely unbearable," said Ward, staring at her furiously. "You yell while the other team is acting; you give ridiculous titles that are patently unfair; you're just generally unpleasant. There's an edge to everything you say." Laura said nothing. "Everyone can feel it," Ward went on. "Everyone feels uncomfortable when you get like that."

Laura got up and went in to the bathroom. She ran the water while she put toothpaste on her brush, so she wouldn't have to listen, but Ward went on, louder.

"You're just so desperate about *winning,*" he called in, ignoring the rush of plumbing. "It makes everyone else feel uncomfortable. I wish you could see yourself when you're up there, interrupting everyone, screaming words out when you're guessing, talking at the top of your lungs . . ."

Laura came back into the bedroom. "I'm sorry," she said to Ward. He stared at her, then yanked the sheet up to his shoulder.

"Unbearable," he said. "God!" He rolled over, away from her.

Laura went around to her side of the bed and slid in under the sheets. Now Ward was facing her unwillingly, his face set in heavy, angry lines. "I'm sorry," she said again, and moved her foot next to his leg. He jerked away from her, as though she were nettles. He rolled away from her again.

"I don't know why you *get* like that," he said, and rolled back to face her again. "How could you possibly think that 'Kaja Gogo' was a legitimate title?"

"Pia and Karin swore it was very popular and that Nat would know it. Anyway, we took it back; we gave you another one." Ward rolled away from her.

"Anyway, I am sorry," Laura said. "You had an awful weekend, and it was my fault."

Ward was silent for a moment. He turned back again. "You think you can act like this all weekend and then just apologize and everything will be all right."

Loosened, finally, from her own rage and pain, unclenching herself from her own point of view, Laura could now see Ward's. She was ashamed. It was a tiny shake of the kaleidoscope; a vastly different pattern.

"I can't think of any other way to start," Laura said. "Tell me what you'd like me to do."

"Don't think you can suddenly turn innocent and placating and make everything all right again," Ward said. He was really angry. "I'm sick of all this chopping and changing. I don't *want* this, Laura. I don't need this in my life. Do you understand that?" He rose up on his elbow and glowered at her.

"I don't blame you," Laura said.

Laura could see how things were. People worked in pairs: when one faltered, the other supported. It had been she, all this time, who had dragged her feet, counting on Ward to carry her weight. Now it was her turn.

Staring at Ward, thinking of this, she saw again the stain on his cheek: faint, ruddy, glowing still. She had hurt Ward: it shamed and thrilled her. It was not something she had known she could do. As though she were changing lenses, as though she had suddenly discovered another light source, she could see now that Ward had no more power over her than she had over him. And her life was her own.

Laura reached out and touched Ward's cheek, very gently. His skin was warm and smooth. She traced the line of the stain. His face, beneath her hand, was mysterious, closed to her. With the sense of freedom came another realization: she could choose Ward or not, herself. It was not only his decision. And, freed, she knew now what she wanted.

"I love you," she said.

But Ward was still angry, his body stiff. For once he would not answer.

"I'm sorry about this weekend," she said again.

"Thank you for apologizing," Ward said. He did not look at her.

"I really mean it," Laura said softly.

Ward pulled away from her and put his head on his hand. "What are you up to?" he asked. "What is really going on?"

"Just what I said," Laura said. "I was so unhappy that I didn't see what I was doing to you. I made a mess of things, and I'm trying to apologize. I really am sorry."

Ward stared at her. "Well, I really am sorry, too," he said, "because I really don't believe you."

There was a long silence between them.

"All I can ask," Laura said finally, "is for you to trust me. But people do change, sometimes—they do grow up—and I'm afraid something like that may be happening to me." She couldn't make him smile. "But I think I've made things very hard on you for a long time, and I don't blame you for being angry, and I think things will be different."

"Why is that?" Ward asked suspiciously.

"Will you marry me?" Laura asked.

It was a risk; it was a definite risk. Laura felt as though she were doing a back dive—that dangerous, irrational plunge into blind space that worked only if you had absolute faith and made your move as brave and reckless as you could. Timidity, a last-minute fear, would bring you down with a crippling fall on the unforgiving board.

Ward looked at her steadily, still angry, but she did not waver. He could not ignore her; he could not roll over once again in a rage. They stared at each other.

She could see he needed her to make another move, to break him out of his sullen state. She traced again the line of her mark on his cheek, then let her finger drift to the side of his head, smoothing his hair back from his temple. She loved the feel of his skin: now, when it might be the last time, she felt it; she longed for Ward's skin, his flesh next to hers; she yearned for it. Oh, please, she thought, let this work.

"Ward, I love you," she said, reminding him, and to her great, great relief she saw his face begin to change. His mouth softened, and she moved her hand to the back of his neck, the thin skin stretched over the fine bones. She did not dare move toward him.

Ward put his hand out to Laura's face. He traced the long line of her neck, and Laura closed her eyes. Ward leaned over her, kissing her first on the mouth, and then on her throat, so gently, so softly, that it seemed as though he might stop, but he did not: he moved down, kissing her shoulders, moving down the length of her, shifting her limbs so he could use them, moving her where he wanted, taking charge of her pleasure and needing her, too, for his own, she could see that now.

Fifteen

In the morning Laura woke to find Ward wrapped closely around her, his body choosing hers. His forearm lay across her shoulder; she put her face next to it and sniffed deeply, closing her eyes. She had been freed from something. She felt light and powerful. Now she could love Ward: how had it seemed risky before? "Fallen in love" was how she felt, gravity-poor, as though depth and distance and weight had altered for her.

The sky beyond the pine trees was a clear, early-morning blue. The thin, white curtains rose, swelled in the uneven breeze, then settled slowly against the wall. Laura lay quite still.

When Ward began to move, she turned in his arms, facing his blurry morning face.

"I love you," she told him at once.

Ward kissed her, his eyes half-shut. "Good," he said, "that's good." He was her friend again, but he had not answered her question.

When Laura went to get Sam up for his sailing lesson, he was still asleep. Sitting down on his bed, she watched him.

One hand was buried beneath the pillow, the other shoved down against the sheet, holding it away from his chest. His chin was raised, his legs sprawled and apart. In sleep he looked utterly committed.

"Sam," she whispered. She touched his shoulder and he moved, turning away from her touch, burrowing his head into the pillow. She put his hand on his other shoulder and gently pushed at it. Sammy shuddered, convulsively, stretching his legs out taut and straight. "Sam," she said softly, "wake up. Time for sailing."

Sam sat up suddenly, his face creased and damp with sleep, breathless. "Where's Daddy?"

"He's gone back to New York. He left early," said Laura. "You were asleep. So was I."

Sam's face was sullen, his flesh soft and rumpled, his eyes heavy-lidded. He scowled. "I want Daddy."

"He had to go to New York to work, Sambo," said Laura. She smoothed his hair away from his forehead. His skin was smooth, faintly damp.

"Why does he have to go to New York? I want him to stay here." Sam's face was thunderous.

"He has to work, Sam—everybody has to work. You have to work—your job is your sailing class, you know. And I don't know where your life jacket is. Do you know where it is?" Laura tried to lead the conversation away from the shoals. Sammy eyed her.

"My life jacket?"

"Because it's not here in your room. I wondered if you had left it someplace else. Did you bring it home last time?"

"Why can't Daddy live with us?"

Laura folded her hands and looked at him.

"Living together is different from visiting," Laura said slowly. "You can like someone very much, you can even love someone, and not want to live with them."

"But I do want to live with Daddy," Sam said crossly.

"Yes, I know," Laura said. She smiled at him. "When you're older, you can. Now you live with me, and you get Ward, too." That was a mistake, she realized at once.

"I don't want Ward," Sam said, furious, his face clotted and dark. "I want Daddy."

Laura stood him up on the bed. "I know that," she said, and began unbuttoning his pajamas. She peeled off the knitted cotton from his chest, creamy white. She put her face against it and blew, making a rude noise. His skin was immaculate, faintly pearly, with a rich, sleepy smell. She blew hard again, and Sammy giggled, unwillingly, and crumpled against her.

"Sam," she whispered, "what I want to know is"—she paused, her mouth at his narrow ear rim—"where did you leave that life jacket?" She shook at his pajama sleeves, pulling them off his soft, knobby arms, jiggling softly at them. "I think you might not have brought it home," she went on, all business. "I think you may have left it at the Fleet, and that black poodle who lives next door may have borrowed it." Sam eyed her. He was standing up now, helping her. "I saw him eyeing it the other day. Poodles are very covetous, you know, and they love life jackets. He might have asked for one for his birthday and not gotten it. He might be very cross that you have one and he doesn't." Laura reached for Sam's jersey, on the bureau. He was listening intently. She continued, very soft and serious, pulling his shirt on over his head, helping with his pants. "Poodles are very tricky, you know, and you have to watch out for them, especially about things like life jackets. And balloons. You know you can't even try to keep a balloon if there are poodles around, because they come and whisper it through the window." Here Sammy came right out and laughed. His face, as she buttoned, smoothed, patted and talked, had grown mild and smooth.

Laura believed this was underhanded, getting over the rough patches this way, but how else did you do it? She hoped he would remember the facts, and gradually let the pain go.

When he was entirely dressed, green-and-brown-and-red-striped jersey, his long blue jeans with rolled-up cuffs, he looked serious and irresistible, and Laura enveloped him, wrapping herself around him. His manhood challenged, Sam struggled to free himself. "Mommy," he complained, and Laura said, "All right," and let him go.

When she came back from taking him to sailing class, Ward was standing out in the driveway washing his new BMW. Laura came up to him from behind and put her arms around him. He was warm from the sun.

"I missed you," she said cheerfully.

"You are weird," Ward said.

"Want some help?" she asked.

"Sorry," Ward said, "this isn't something women can do. Their pelvises are the wrong shape."

He was sliding a stream of water over the car, a slow, liquid lashing, a crystal snake. "No kibbitzing," he said; "there's an art to this."

"I'll just watch, then," Laura said, and sat down on the stone wall. Ward played the hose back and forth across the hood, glistening dark blue in the sun. "I can see it's tricky," she said.

Ward eyed her. "This technique has been passed down in our family through the generations."

"I bet no one taught Jeanie," Laura said. Jeanie was Ward's younger sister, whose state of rebellion had been nearly continual, though she had finally left the Hare Krishnas and joined the Mary Kay Cosmetic Company.

"Jeanie," said Ward, "no. Dad didn't teach Jeanie."

"Does your father speak to Jeanie? Does she ever come home?"

Ward covered the whole car, and the sliding surface was a liquid shimmer in the sun. He brought the bucket over closer and plunged the big sponge into the soapy water.

"She comes home," he said. "She even came home when she was a Krishna. She brought her boyfriend."

"Another Krishna?"

Ward nodded. "He told them his name was Krishna Vey. So my parents called him Krishna Vey and her Oy Vey. Jeanie said they had to sleep in the same room. The next morning Dad went in and found Jeanie asleep in her bed and Krishna Vey curled up on the rug underneath the window. Dad told them they might spend their whole lives singing and dancing, but they had no idea of how to have fun."

Laura laughed. "I can imagine my father telling one of my boyfriends that he should be sleeping with me."

"She was twenty-five or so by then," Ward said. "I think they would have settled for a shred of normality, any shred."

"What happens now? Does he yell at her?"

"Oh, sure. He yells at her, then it's all over. He's crazy about her. When she called up to tell him she was joining the Krishnas, he said, 'Good. Get settled into something regular, maybe you'll start calling home once a week.' "

"Amazing," Laura said.

"No, it's not," Ward said. "What choice do parents have? They can't finally turn against their children."

"Mine would have," Laura said.

"Baloney," Ward said. "You never dared find out. Of course they wouldn't."

"Me?" Laura said. "I was famous. I was famously rebellious."

"Oh, right," Ward said mildly. "You went to Mummy's boarding school, then on to a nice college, then married the Princeton boy."

"Dropped out of the college, which was avant-garde and

pinko, got married when I was still a minor and had to be signed over from my father to Nat, like a ward of the court. Imagine anyone being signed into Nat's care!"

"Very rebellious," Ward said, "from daughter to chattel." He was squatting at the grille, and the soapy water was sliding past his hands in great, soft foamy cakes.

"I got caught for smoking in eighth grade," Laura offered. Ward turned and smiled at her.

Now that she thought of it, Laura could not remember a real confrontation with her father. Once when she was twelve she had said "Damn" where he could hear her, but she hadn't meant to. She had stopped breathing when she realized he was there, and she had tiptoed violently away, hoping he would think it was someone else, some ambient sound from another community of beings, and not a forbidden swearword from his youngest daughter.

"Once I said 'Damn,' almost right in front of him," Laura told Ward.

Ward whistled admiringly. "I take it all back." Laura smiled at him.

"Okay," she said, "I wasn't a famous rebel. No one rebelled against my father."

"Nope. Had you all buffaloed," said Ward. "See, you do the other end next. It's a sequence."

Buffaloed, Laura thought. It was a strange word to use about her father: thin-lipped, precise, controlled.

Ward dragged the heavy loops of the hose to the other end of the car.

"You're awfully good at this," Laura called to him. "You should do it professionally."

"And what should you do professionally?" Ward called back.

"What do you think?" Laura leaned back on the stone wall and raised her face to the sky. Inside the darkness of her closed eyelids, she felt the sun's hot, red presence. She wished Sheba were there, carefully licking her matte-gray fur, stroking herself into chic. Laura opened her eyes.

"Ward, what *do* you think I should do?"

Ward came back around the car. "First your hair, then your nails."

"Stop."

"Just do more. Take more pictures. Take more courses. Teach. Just go into it."

"But I'm scared of teaching."

"I know that."

"Well?"

Ward shrugged his shoulders. "Well, nothing. It should be something you do because you want to. Then it won't scare you so much. You asked, I told you."

"Mmm," Laura said. She leaned back against the wall. It sounded right. Ward vanished behind the car again.

"Don't watch this part," he called. "This is the part only my father knows."

"I'm coming around, I'm warning you," Laura said, and came to stand behind him. "There's no reason for you to know things I don't," she said.

"Get out of here, this is a family secret."

"Ward, did you ever fight with your father?"

Ward snorted. "Did I?"

"No, but I mean one real one. A serious confrontation."

"Well, there was one, I guess, but neither of us knew it at the time." Ward was scrubbing the fenders with the sponge. "My father used to hit me all the time. I don't mean he used to beat me, but he used to give me these little punches, love taps, little cuffs. He'd do it if he was pleased, he'd do it when he was mad at me. It was all-purpose. I'd come into the kitchen and he'd be standing there and he'd say, 'Hey, Tiger' and he'd give me a cuff on the shoulder." Ward put the sponge deep into the bucket and squeezed. "When I was little I didn't mind. I didn't think I had any right to mind: that was what my dad did, he hit me all the time." Ward started on the fender again, his forearm brown and dry against the slick glimmer of the chrome. "And Dad's very grabby, he was always putting his arms around me and kissing me."

"Your father?" said Laura. She could not imagine her father kissing his children, ever.

Ward smiled at her. "We used to have a joke: Dad can't talk to something he can't touch. He's gotta have his hand on it. Anyway, I didn't mind when I was little, but when I started to grow up, it started to irritate me. When I'd come into a room and he'd go for me, I'd swerve to stay out of range. Then he'd come after me. He was relentless. We got kind of tense about it, but it slackened off, for some reason, when I went away to boarding school. He hadn't gone to boarding school, so for a while I was a slightly awesome figure. He backed off a little bit. Then when I went to Columbia, he started up again. He had gone to college, himself. I was back being his kid again. He started in on me again and nearly drove me nuts.

"One day I was sitting in the kitchen with my mother, and Dad came in and sat down at the table next to me. He leaned his arms on the table, folded, and his hand was right next to my arm. He started talking to me, and every time he ended a sentence he'd give me a poke. 'Right, Ward?' he'd say, *poke.* 'What do you think?' *poke.* He knew, and he didn't know, what he was doing. I lost track completely of what he was saying; I was just waiting for the next poke. I slid my chair over so I was further away from him, and he slid his over next to mine. He put one arm across my shoulder and started punching my arm with the other. His face was right *there.*" Ward held up the dripping sponge an inch before his nose. "I felt as though I were about to go crazy. I had the feeling that this great leering face and punching fist had got me trapped forever. I felt as though I couldn't breathe."

Ward had the sponge in both hands. He was sitting on his heels, his face was fierce and funny.

"Then my father started to punch my arm again, and I reached both hands and I grabbed his fist. I grabbed it in both hands and I squeezed it." Ward raised the sponge in his hands and squeezed, the soft fibers collapsing in his grip, the soap sliding down his wrists and forearms.

"I squeezed it as though I was trying to choke it to death. I was wild: I could feel what it would be like to murder someone. I throttled it. God!" Ward shook his head. "I was crazy. I yelled at my father, 'Keep your fucking hands to yourself!' I had never said anything like that to him in my life. I was shaking and blazing. I would have killed him."

"And what did he do?"

"He just stared at me. He didn't fight my hands, he didn't pull away. Then he started to pat my shoulder with his other hand, then he took both his hands away from me, and then he moved his chair away from me. He looked at my mother. 'Okay, pal,' he said, without looking at me.

"I sat there, wild, waiting for something more. I couldn't believe what I'd done. I couldn't stand it. I felt as though I had murdered him. I yanked back my chair and stormed out of the room, slammed the door, crashed up the stairs. I went into my room and slammed that door. I sat down on the bed. I just sat there, feeling terrible, as though I'd killed my father, waiting for something else to happen. But it was over. I lay down and stared at the ceiling. What I kept thinking, what was so awful, was that his hand had just rested in mine."

Ward put his hands back in the bucket, slowly filling the sponge with the soapy water.

"He hadn't tried to fight me. And his hand was so weak. All that time I'd been thinking of him as this huge muscle man, this guy who could kill me with one of his pokes." He looked at Laura and shook his head. "I could have broken his hand off at the wrist, it was so frail. I could have done anything I'd wanted to him. Anything," he said helplessly.

Laura smiled at him; she could feel his remembered shame. Strange how the most shameful act is the one that sets you free: her own desperate strike at Ward's face.

"So," Ward said, bending again over the car, "that's the story. Real Life Drama."

"A revelation," Laura said.

"How a revelation?"

"Wasps don't yell at each other. In my family we never yelled at each other. If someone did, it was like a nuclear bomb exploding: weeks of silent repercussions. Shame. Despair. Terrible damage."

"You never yelled at your parents? They never yelled at you?"

"Are you crazy?"

"*I'm* not."

Laura laughed. "Silence and terror: it's not the ideal formula, is it? Still, it must have some merit—here we all still are, walking around by the hundreds, supporting L. L. Bean."

"Stiff upper lip," Ward said. "Puritan virtues. Those aren't ours."

Laura went back. "But what happened, after you'd grabbed your father's hand, when you came downstairs?"

"I don't remember exactly. I said I was sorry for yelling at him. And he said, 'No, no, you're not a kid anymore. I forget that.' "

"He said that? He apologized?"

Ward smiled again. "He's a world-class pop."

Ward seemed so easily to have found the right way to look at his parents; it seemed so obvious, so simple, hearing him talk. Laura found the words from Karin's song in her mind: *Don't stand, don't stand, don't stand so close to me.* She wondered how far you had to be from your parents to see what they were really like. Ward seemed to be at just the right distance, but she herself had no sense of her parents as real people:

they were magnified, bleary shapes seen from too close, as Ward's father's face had been, looming next to him at the table.

Now that her own private kaleidoscope had made that slight, revelatory shift, her memories looked different. What if her father had been—instead of cold, censorious, impenetrable—merely knotted up in his own emotions, hiding his own fears? What if he had needed a poke in the arm, fierce insistence, from his children, on love? What if she had imagined the constant threat of abandonment, disdain?

Rage and fear, Laura thought: they muffled everything. But listening to Ward, holding on to what Richie had told her, she perceived a gradual clearing. The landscape around her was altering.

Laura looked around, thinking again of the cat.

"Ward," she said, "I miss Sheba."

Ward was crouching now by the wheel, rubbing at the hubcap, and he put his arm around her ankles. "Don't feel bad," he said. "Don't."

His arm felt good. Laura liked the simplicity.

Richie ambled out to the driveway, his hands stuffed into his pockets, his shirt open at the neck. He looked at Ward's arm locked around Laura's legs.

"You've caught one, I see," he said. He looked Laura up and down. "Quite a good one, too."

"I'm too young," Laura said, stepping out of Ward's circle. "He'll only have to throw me back."

Ward shook his head, working at the chrome. "The trouble with your sister-in-law," he said, "is that she thinks she's going to be a nymphet for the rest of her life."

"Am I old?" Laura asked.

"Next year thirty," Ward said dolorously; "after that it's all downhill."

"Oh, buzz off," Laura said. "I was asked for my I.D. in a bar last year. That meant they thought I was under twenty-one."

"Well, they won't next year," Ward said. "All that is over."

Laura looked at Richie. "Ward's jealous," she said.

"God," Ward said, "if people thought I were twenty years old, I wouldn't last one day in my business."

"Oh, all right," said Laura, "you win. I won't be young forever. I'll start being something else."

Richie yawned, a sudden, inward swoop. "Well," he said, "I'm going to make a trip into Bar Harbor this afternoon. Nose around for my church."

"I saw it last week," Laura announced.

"You saw it?" Riche said.

"Just for a minute," Laura said. "I couldn't get it to stop."

Richie nodded and stuck his arms out in a diagonal stretch. "*When will I see you again,*" he sang. Laura looked at his hands, big gentle shapes half-opened against the deep sky. There was a picture, she thought; and remembered Ward's hands, squeezing the sponge as though he were choking his father: another one. What about hands, she thought, a series of hand portraits? She liked the idea of it, the shapes and gestures that hands took on, their angles, their tensions. Subtler than faces—would it be too subtle, too abstract? It would have to be people she knew, moments she understood. She would have to come out of hiding, carry her camera around her neck, focus, making loud, judgmental clicks, intruding on people's lives. She had never done that. The mask sequence had been mostly shots of strangers—people on the street with extraordinary sunglasses or veiled hats, or people lying in full sun, their faces shaded somehow. They were scenes that involved timing and focus and a sort of visual knack, but no knowledge of the people, no explanations, no intrusions. This would be quite different.

Laura forgot herself, standing in the sunlight between the two men on the driveway, the gleaming car before them, the slippery soap foaming across the shining metal, the men's voices a comfortable blur in her ears. She thought of shutter speeds and focusing, a choice of lenses. Portraits of gestures: oh, she liked it.

Now, Ward stood up. "The Final Rinse," he said, and went off to turn on the hose again. Near Laura's feet the hose came to sudden, liquid life, the flooding surge sinking instantly among the stones. Richie looked at his battered black Volvo station wagon, next to the BMW. The Volvo had a film of gray dust over it, and it was parked at a crazy angle, its nose thrusting eagerly over the low stone wall at the edge of the driveway, as though it were contemplating a wild leap into the trees. The hubcaps were battered and rusty, and there were dents in the fenders and a long, narrow streak along one side.

"I must be doing something wrong," Richie said, cocking his head at it.

"It's a nice car," Laura said, "and it says exactly who you are."

"New England quasi-intellectual liberal," said Richie.

"In a word," Laura said.

Ward began to rinse the BMW. Magically, the silver ribbon of water cleared the white suds, slithering them without resistance over the curved sides of the car, laying them in vanishing clouds on the stones. The car, beneath the layer of brilliance, gleamed in the sun, light reflecting off each shallow ripple in its surface, shining like an advertisement.

"Who does that say Ward is?" Richie asked.

"Mafia lawyer trying to look straight," Laura said.

"Hey," Ward said, turning the hose in her direction.

"Sorry," she said. "Brilliant young New York lawyer, on the rise."

Ward nodded. "That's it."

"Would you tell me if you were in the Mafia?"

"Maybe," said Ward. "It would depend. Do you like cement overshoes?"

"That's not funny," said Laura.

The car was finished and it stood before them, perfect in the clear sunlight. When it dried, the sheen would diminish: this was its moment of flawless radiance, before the three of them.

"It does look nice," said Laura. "I wish I knew how to wash a car like that."

"If you married into the right family," Ward said severely, "you might learn."

"Well," said Richie, "enough of this. I'm going down to pick up Pia; I'll get Sammy, too. Find out what the news is from the rest of the world."

But he did not move. The three of them stood still in the sun, unwilling to lose the moment of glittering brilliance: the BMW, dazzling and surreal next to the battered Volvo; the deep secretive pines edging the lawn, the restless glimmer of the harbor far beyond, and the clear, singing air. Laura, motionless, felt the sun beating into her, as though it were melting something at her center. She closed her eyes, but the vivid brilliance of the car, the two solid shapes flanking her, stayed on as afterimages in the hot darkness.

Sixteen

The weather held for the rest of the month. A few rainy days, a few dense with fog, reminded everyone of where they were, but, for the most part, the days were long and clear. The woman at the Pine Tree Market, packing Laura's bag of groceries, told her she had never seen such a July, and, down at the Fleet, the comfortable college boy who ran it told Laura he'd never had so few knot-tying days. This year's group, he said, had barely heard of the rabbit coming out of its hole and around the tree: the bowline.

The mornings were chilly, and the tops of the pine trees stood stiff and pale with early mist. Thick, white vapor filled the harbor, but by midmorning it was gone. By midday, out of the wind it was hot, the sun a steady presence in the thin air, the sky a solemn blue above. Out in the sound, the boats slid brashly through the bright water, vanishing behind the trim, green-stacked islands stiff with trees, and reappearing beyond them, their bright spinnakers bellied out before them, the wind tearing wildly at the sails.

Karin began talking about the boy at the take-out window at the Docksider Restaurant. He was going to Amherst in the fall, she said. She was out every night, and Laura, curious, went to the Docksider one evening to get steamers for dinner from the famous Justin.

When she gave her name for the order, he said at once, "You must be the famous aunt." He was round-faced and cheerful, with good manners and one, thin, gold earring. Laura was surprised: she had expected someone with a Mohawk haircut and a poisonous style.

"I'm the aunt, anyway," she said. "I know you're Justin."

Justin folded his arms on the high counter. "That's me," he said, and smiled.

"Well, how do you like seafood?" Laura asked.

"I hope I never see another lobster again," Justin said, shaking his head. "This has done me for lobsters forever, I think." He looked past Laura. "Here's Rin," he said.

Karin was coming in the door with a small girl, potbellied and blond, with enormous, flat, blue eyes.

"Hi, Jus," said Karin, "hi Laura." She had dropped the "aunt," Laura noticed, and found she was pleased.

Karin turned to the child. "Can you make it up onto the bench?" She knelt easily and put her arms around the little girl, lifting her onto the bench at the outdoor table. "This is Schuyler Wainwright," she said. "Schuyler, this is my aunt Laura, and you know Justin." Schuyler Wainwright stared bluely at them. She was wearing a bright-pink bathing suit and a pair of elastic-topped shorts covered with red elephants.

"I like your elephants," Laura offered, but Schuyler was not impressed. Karin sat down next to the child, her hip easing comfortably against the fat, small legs.

"We've been at the pool all afternoon," she explained. "We're a little bagged out. We have trouble talking a lot when we're this bagged out." She smoothed the thin, wispy blond hair away from Schuyler's face, then leaned back.

"Well, Schuy?" she asked. "What are we going to have for dinner? Are we having hamburgers?"

Schuyler was at last moved to contribute: she shook her head.

"Are we having fried clams?" Justin asked. Schuyler shook her head, ducking her fat chin against her neck. She still looked watchful and solemn.

"Are we having—" Karin paused, as though she were racking her brains, but Laura could see that this was a ritual for the three of them. They knew each other, Karin and Justin and Schuyler; they had made a pattern that included each other easily and kindly. Justin and babysitting had given Karin access to another part of life, an entry into the larger world. Affluence and independence, responsibility and freedom, had altered everything, expanded her landscape.

"Are we having *grilled cheese sandwiches?*" Karin asked, the question filled with suspense. At this, Schuyler's face suddenly dissolved into a radiant, embarrassed smile, and she spoke.

"Yes," she said clearly, and, to compensate for her boldness, she crossed her small, thick legs tightly, at the ankle.

Karin clapped her hands and turned to Justin, her face lit up. It was her own life she was now living.

Pia had become a sailor. She had joined the Fleet, and went out on the water every day. She crewed in the races, and talked shyly about tactics, at meals. She spent the long afternoons out on boats with friends, and mentioned islands and harbors that Laura had never heard of. She learned about the intricacies of wind, of leverage and strain, spinnakers and Genoa jibs. She came home flushed and windblown, clean of anxieties.

Ward drifted in and out.

"Ward?" Laura would say, when he stepped into the silent room, thick with darkness and her presence. She wrapped her arms around him, breathing in his dense, tired smell.

"How is it?" he asked.

"Like airplanes," she answered. "Get into bed and rub it off."

"That was my plan," Ward said.

Richie spent the days with his sketch pad and camera: Mount Desert Island was full of Beaux Arts design, grand summer cottages. Often Sarah went with him, sitting quietly in the grass while he sketched or photographed. She was making a quilt, and carried with her a bag of her family's old clothes, clean and soft and worn. She cut pieces out carefully, against a neat cardboard pattern, an octagon. It would be like a family album, she told Laura, a record of them all moving through their lives.

There were not, really, so many weeks in a month. By the last week, Laura felt as though she had been in the house only a few days. She had spent her mornings in the darkroom. She went up as soon as Sammy was at sailing class, and worked steadily, blissfully, the hours passing silently in a dark stream. She lapsed into the rhythm of the printing—the slowness of it, the dreamy, magical process of liquids and images. She liked the sour smell, the subtle privacy of the red light; she liked watching the image come glimmering up at her from the empty, white paper. She liked working toward a moment of clarity. She kept the contrasts of the tree pictures faint; she wanted the precise and geometric patterns to be after-images, ghostly trees remembered by the retina.

In the afternoons, aside from the time she spent with Sammy, she had begun the hand series. The more she thought of it, the more she liked it. She wanted children's hands next to parents, genetic patterns shown; she wanted the soft, un-touched shapes, smooth and rounded, next to the parents'—strong, gnarled, knotty at the joints, shaped by the angles of their lives. And she wanted gestures: Sarah's neat, controlling circles, Richie's generous sweeps ending nowhere, Ward's perpendicular slices.

Laura looked at her own hands, examining them one morning in the dim, red light. They were stained with developing fluid, angular in the unnatural shadows, strange and livid. Shaped and colored by her profession: she liked that. Then, what about Sammy, what about being a mother? The tension between the two versions of herself now exhilarated her. She liked the pull between them. After delivering Sammy to the Fleet every morning, she was ready, eager, for the solitary darkness, the incipient images. After a morning of silence, she was ready again to see him at lunch. She felt herself rich and fortunate, with two conflicting centers to her life.

The prints of trees now covered the wall in the bedroom. They presented their neat, intricate patterns, impossibly sophisticated. Laura stood in the room with the door shut and appraised them, her hands clasped in front of her. This was what she had meant to say.

On the nights when Ward was there, he slept with his arms close around her, as though she were ballast for him against the shifting tides of sleep; as though she were precious. He still had not answered Laura's question, and there was a waiting distance between them, but no coolness. Laura felt her own certainty growing, during the month, her anxieties lessening. She felt a moment would come.

Sailing lessons ended in the last week. The July people were packing up. Pia, Sam and Karin were all free. The last two days would be spent cleaning the house, and Laura planned a picnic just before, a last treat, a swan song.

Seventeen

The day they had chosen was damp and foggy in the early morning, but by the time they loaded the boat, near noon, the sky was cloudless. The sun was dazzling on the dark water, and the wind was strong. The light slanted more each day; the summer was withdrawing. They all wore windbreakers and sweaters for the picnic.

Once clear of the harbor, Ward opened up the throttle as they came around the point, and the boat began to skim like a skipped stone. Ward's flannel shirt flapped wildly, and Sarah's kerchief struggled to get loose from her hair. Laura tightened her arms and folded them across her chest against the wind. Pia, watching, folded hers in exactly the same way. There was something impossibly glamorous about Laura, Pia felt: she could duplicate the gesture but not the style. She leaned into the wind at the same angle as her aunt's, her arms clenched over her chest.

Laura caught her eye and smiled.

"Cold?" she yelled, and Pia nodded, though she was not. "You're like me," Laura said, and put her hands on Pia's arms and rubbed them hard, the rough chafing bringing the blood up. Pia smiled, her face stiff with the wind. "Thanks," she yelled back, cheered.

As they passed the small islands, heading toward the Western Way, the old houses on them stood out against the trees and sky. Their walls and roofs were of lichen-gray shingle, their doors and windows trimmed with white. They stood moored in seas of rippling grass, as though the earth were no more substantial than the tidal swell beside it. The strong northern light slanted against them, picking out the white-trimmed sills, showing each building alone in its surroundings, solitary against the sky, above the sea.

Laura rubbed at Pia's shoulders, wrapping her body easily around the child's. Pia's thin, supple shape had become familiar to her; Laura no longer felt the anxious strangeness she had with the two girls. Sammy was sitting with Richie, his puffy orange life jacket swollen around his torso, muffling his chin. Laura waved at him.

They roared down the Western Way, the boat slapping against the waves. No one tried to speak over the noise of the wind and the engine. Ship's Island came into view—low, bare and rocky—and Ward slowed the motor, changing its lunging roar to a subdued, diminished tone. Ward had told them this used to be a stop on the Lewiston steamer route, but Laura could not imagine it. The island was tiny and did not have the look of an island that had ever had houses on it. There was too much wind, and no cover. Where would those ladies boarding the steamers have stepped, in their deep-ruffled skirts, with their primly held parasols? This rising slope of granite cobblestones, rocks washed smooth and serene against the shoreline boulders, the harsh mineral sand?

They beached the boat, Ward yanking the motor out of the water at the last moment, the boat wallowing widely, sinking into the shallow depths at once, the hull scraping faintly on the pebbles at the water's edge. They clambered out, their pants rolled up, and floundered through the waves to the wide stretch of sand that curved in a long half-moon against the water. Richie held his arms out for Sammy, who preferred to jump himself but was finally daunted by the relative depths of the chilling water. Richie carried him, embarrassed, to the edge.

Sea gulls rose up into the high blue of the sky, screaming, their agitated wings angling against the wind. As they straggled toward the land the birds did not disperse, but wheeled overhead, their cries shrill and raucous.

"Maybe they're nesting," Sarah said. "If they are we shouldn't stay here." She and Karin walked up into the long dune grass to look for nests. Their silhouettes were dark against the sky: Karin's flapping blue jean jacket, loose at the cuffs, the neat curve of its bottom belling out at Karin's waist, hair streaming haphazardly from both their heads. They turned, finally, and waved for the others to come up; there were no nests.

Sammy labored up the hill beside Laura, carrying a thermos. They stopped at the top of the sandy slope, and Laura shook out the blanket in the wind. The sun beat down on her head, and the brown roughness of the wool flapped against her legs.

" 'U.S. Army,' " Pia read. "Why do you have an Army blanket?"

"It's from when Nat was in the reserves. I think his little lunch box is still around, too; all those neat tiny knives and forks and spoons and canteens. The Army stuff is terrific for picnics, much better than the stuff from Abercrombie's."

"The little lunch box is otherwise known as a mess kit," said Ward.

"Mess kit sounds so disgusting," Laura pointed out. "Like something you get for a traveling cat."

"Traveling cat?" said Ward. "Did you say 'traveling cat'?" He struck a dramatic pose, his arms out like a sorcerer. He sang two minor chords: "*Da dum:* The Last Journey."

Laura looked at Sammy. "Do you think Ward is funny? He thinks he is funny."

But Sammy was still with the blanket. "Was that my daddy's?" he asked. Laura nodded. "Then why do you have it?"

Laura shrugged. "I don't know. I just do. I don't think he wanted it. We each ended up with odds and ends. He has some things of mine, too."

"I think you should have given that back to my daddy," Sam said belligerently. "I think you should give it back to him now."

"Sambo," Laura said, squatting down next to him in the sand. "We've settled things between us. We're not going to go on trading things back and forth. Now we're separate."

Sammy was not looking at her. He was digging a hole in the sand with his heel.

"Are you married to my daddy?" he asked. He was churning at the sand, and chunks of dark, sea-damp sludge were being thrown up, spattering his sneakers and Laura's.

"I am in a way," Laura said, "but it's not a real way."

"Then why don't you live with him?" Sammy asked.

"That's why it isn't a real way. We're separated now. We won't live together anymore."

Sammy glanced up at her sideways, unfriendly. His hair rose suddenly with the wind in a shiny fan above his forehead, then fell. Laura reached toward him and he broke away abruptly, running up the beach toward the dune grass, his arms stretched out high and stiff from his sides.

Above them, the gulls still cried and shrilled, swooping and diving in the wild currents. But the picnickers now ignored the birds, dragging baskets, blankets, towels and thermoses across the sand, spreading out and settling down. The gulls screamed overhead like demons, wheeling and crossing in the air like a torment.

They spread the food out on the blanket, a small feast.

Salami, cheddar and mozzarella cheese, heart-red local tomatoes, limp, frilly lettuce, mayonnaise and mustard, fresh brown bread that Sarah had made, deviled eggs, plums and pears, and thermoses of iced tea and lemonade. Spread out across the rough brown blanket, against the stony beach, it looked like a miracle in the wilderness. They stretched out on the sand and ate.

"Does anyone mind if I have the last deviled egg?" Ward asked. "It's only my sixth." Laura made a pig noise deep in her throat, and passed the egg to him.

"Ka-*reen,*" Richie said, "*what* is that you're eating?"

They all looked at Karin, who held a sandwich.

"Toe-cheese," suggested Pia, but the joke was old.

"Salami," Karin admitted.

"Salami," said Ward, scandalized and delighted. "Did you ever see a salami, with its soft white coat and its big brown eyes? What did it ever do to you?"

Karin stuck out her tongue, and Laura said, "Be quiet," to Ward, and then to Karin, "But why did you change?"

Karin shrugged her shoulders placidly. "I don't know. I just got bored by vegetables. They aren't that interesting." She sat cross-legged on the sand, in her jeans jacket over an old, green turtleneck and baggy Army pants. Her hair streamed in a complicated web around her face. She seemed smooth as a millpond, as though a sudden wind had never jangled her surface into a rough, choppy glitter.

Laura turned to Sammy, hoping for the same friendly calm. Sammy was sitting with his legs straight out in front of him on the blanket. He was tearing tiny pieces off his peanut butter sandwich and putting them in his mouth, gazing sternly out toward the water.

"How you doing, Sambo?" Laura asked, but he only nodded slowly, without looking at her. He looked unrelated to the rest of them, sprawled easily on the ground, with their faces turned toward each other, responsive.

Later, Sarah and Laura began packing up the food, rinsing out the sticky plastic glasses, burying the fruit pits in the sand, hurling crusts and tidbits toward the dunes. The others drifted down to the water's edge; they started skimming stones. Stepping around the waves, bent awkwardly at the waist and stooping in the shallow water, they looked like ungainly wading birds, some strange wingless giant cranes.

"I wish I'd brought my quilt," Sarah said, when they had finished.

"It's too windy," Laura said.

"Well, I can't just *sit* here," Sarah said, smiling.

"It's too cold for swimming, even for you," Laura told her. "Let's take a walk." They stood up, dusting sand from their jeans, and started down the long, curved beach. The sky had streaks of gray in it now, and the wind was beginning to come up. They walked along the edge of the waves, where the green translucent ripples sank into the porous sand with a hiss, leaving a curve of foamy rime. Laura stopped to roll up her pants. The waves were icy on her bare ankles. The wet cloth resisted, and she left the folded legs ragged and uneven and kicked her way through the lapping waves. Overhead the sea gulls still wheeled and cried. At the end of the half-moon curve, they stopped. Behind them, the blanket on the beach and the group of figures at the water's edge seemed inconsequential. The bright colors and flapping edges suggested something casual that the water might have tossed up, that the sea gulls dropped. Beyond Laura and Sarah, a mound of granite boulders lay in a broad tangle above the high-water line.

The big, smooth rocks rose from the pale sand like ancient animals, broad, seamed, massive. Laura and Sarah climbed across them until they found a gap like a foxhole, room for both of them among the pink curves of stone. They sat down, their bodies protected from the wind. Their heads were above the rest of the rocks, and they could see the others, far down the beach. The sand beneath them, sheltered from the wind, was warm.

"This is nice," Sarah said, "warm." She leaned against the roughened stone. "The wind's come up."

"Are you cold?" Laura asked. "I never think of you as being cold. I think of you up there in New Hampshire in the winter—I could never do it. I get cold in bed with a quilt and a hot-water bottle and Ward. I always wait for him to get into bed first."

"Oh, New Hampshire," Sarah said dismissively. "That's not a choice. It's what there is." She smiled at the cold bed. "Ward's nice. I bet he always does get into bed first."

"He does," Laura said; "he always does. He *is* nice."

"Well," Sarah said, "*are* you going to get married?"

Laura smiled but shook her head. "I don't know." She was superstitious, and would not claim something before it was fact.

"But what does that mean?" Sarah asked. "Are you just going to stay together until something happens, one way or the other?"

It was how Laura had felt before. "No," she said now, "we'll decide things pretty soon. I want to get started."

"On?"

"Everything," Laura said. "Work, where I live—my Life." She smiled at her sister. "But things are going well between us."

From where they sat, they looked out at another island curving toward their own. It was uninhabited, too, but more imposing than theirs; it rose to a gentle spine along the center, with pine trees along it in a vivid green crest. Between the two islands the water lay flat, a layer of deep green gray that wrinkled in the sun and rippled intricately in the wind.

"What do you mean, though, New Hampshire's not a choice?" Laura asked.

"I used to think I would order my life according to things

I could control. That we'd choose where we wanted to live, the sort of things we did. But now I see how amazingly limited my choices are. And I love New Hampshire, I really do. I love the house, and I love those mountains."

The image of the mountains rose, the high slopes, the dim, purple silhouette, the sense of vast and benign presence.

"Is Richie happy there?" Laura asked.

Sarah sighed. "I don't know. I hope so. If it were me, I'd do it differently. I think he's wasting himself there. I think he's breaking his heart as an architect, but he loves the place. He loves living in that countryside. But he gets so sad, sometimes."

"And?" said Laura, "then what do you do?"

"Oh, it depends. Sometimes I can't do anything. The winters are awfully long. And sometimes I can do a lot for him." She smiled at Laura. "We know each other pretty well."

"You're happy together?"

Sarah nodded. "We're happy, I think so. We're married to each other. There are times, I think, when the idea of love has nothing to do with things, when you don't love each other. But it's a commitment; it gives a shape to your life, and the love comes back, if you hold on."

"But you do love each other?"

"Yes. Sometimes I think what it would be to live alone, but it's like a scene in a movie, not real. A tiny, white room. I don't ever imagine I could get there."

"Do you and Richie fight?"

"What is this?" Sarah asked. "Are you conducting a survey? Do you and Ward fight?"

"Ward and I had the most terrible fight of all time, I thought," Laura said. "I thought nothing could possibly survive a fight like this. It's done, I thought, I thought I'd killed the whole thing."

"Was it when Nat came up?"

"Yes. You know what happened? Ward slapped me in the face."

But Sarah did not seemed shocked. "People do awful things when they're fighting."

"Well, I thought that was the end of the world, not only because it was something you should never do, but because I thought I would never forgive him, once he'd done it. I knew I'd use it against him, forever; I'd poison things with it. It was too big an advantage for me to have."

"And? What did you do?"

"I slapped *him* in the face, so we were even!" Laura said, and they both began to laugh. Laura hugged her knees. Beyond them, the channel went suddenly crosshatched and glittering. Things were more radical than Laura had imagined before, more erratic, more wildly fluctuating. At the same time, they were more stable; those wild swings tended toward dead center again. It was comforting to know.

When they finally stood up, the wind caught them hard in the face, and the sleeves of Laura's sweater flapped suddenly like banners. The tide was coming in, and the big pink-granite rocks were being slowly surrounded by the lapping intrusion of the waves. Walking back down the beach, they watched the others, who were still down by the water's edge, skipping stones. As they came closer they heard the others give a shout, and Laura and Sarah broke into a jog, their feet splashing in the shallow, frigid water, the cold wind gusting in their faces.

Pia, her arm a casual sideways swivel, had tossed a stone loosely across the water, skipping it across the ridges of the waves like a smocking needle across gathered fabric. The stone had skipped fifteen times, twenty-five: no one had ever seen a stone skip like that. Sammy was roused to fever pitch.

"Watch!" he shouted, and threw his stone as far as he could, hurling it into a high and clumsy arc; it fell heavily into the water. Karin, jealous, threw two more stones and quit. Ward and Richie stood carefully, Pia's example before them, and poised their arms, tensing their whole bodies, hefting the stones judiciously before they threw. No one could match it. Pia, her hands stuck into her jacket, grinned at them all, as though a small miracle had been performed.

They picked up the blankets and packed up the baskets. Ward collected the thermoses.

"The Last Picnic," he said solemnly.

"It is," Laura said. She picked up the Army blanket and shook it out. "Have you had a good time in Maine?" she asked. "Are you glad I invited you?"

Ward laughed. "I'm glad you invited me," he said. He took the other side of the blanket, and the two of them stood with the dark, coarse blanket stretched between them. They flapped it slowly up and down in the wind. The air above them was tumultuous, full of noise and motion. The crusts and crumbs flew up into the air as though freed, as though they were part of the tumult, as though Ward's and Laura's shared gestures were magic, setting things free, releasing them into the singing wind, the rowdy heights above.

When they were finished, they stepped toward each other, hands raised as in a dance. Carefully matching the corners, Laura took the blanket, and Ward put his arms around her as she folded it up into a neat square. Laura felt his arms wrap across her shoulders, felt the warmth of him against the wind.

"Were you serious about that?" Ward whispered.

Laura felt Sam's head butt heavily against her thigh. Distracted, she reached down to pull his head to her, but he pulled away.

"About what?" she asked, leaning away to grab Sammy, but Ward would not let her go.

"Your question," he said.

"*Mother,*" Sammy said insistently.

Laura smiled at Ward. "I was," she said. "Ouch, stop it, Sammy. Don't punch me." She leaned over again, but he stood rigid and demanding in front of her. "Now what is it?" They stood waiting, Ward's arms still around her, Sammy sullen. He would not look at them. Laura turned back to Ward.

"I was, yes," she said. "Were you?"

"I want to show my mother something," Sammy said loudly.

"In a minute," Laura said, watching Ward's face.

"About my question?" Ward asked.

"Yes."

"*Now!*" Sammy yelled, kicking sand at both of them.

"Yes," said Ward.

"*Sammy,*" Laura said, angry, and reached out to take him by the shoulders. He pulled away from her and ran toward the water. Behind her, Ward picked up the blanket and the last basket. When she caught up with Sam, he stared up at her sideways, hostile and stubborn.

"Don't interrupt, and don't kick sand," she said severely. "Now, what did you want to show me?"

Sam, his face resentful, held up a small rock. Laura took it: it was unremarkable, a mottled pink and brown with an uneven surface. Laura looked at Sam.

"Thank you, Sam. But why did you want to show it to me?" She held it out on her palm. Sam, without speaking, took it and threw it down the beach defiantly.

"Your shoelaces are untied," Laura said. It was said as a threat, and Sammy ducked his head and ran insolently down to the water's edge, where the others were loading the things and climbing on board.

Laura swung herself up, and Ward climbed on with the anchor, pushing the boat with a swish out into the deeper water. He stood next to the engine, but, before turning on the motor, he picked up Sam's life jacket.

"Here you go, Sam," he said.

Sammy climbed past him toward the bow, without looking at him. "Hey," Ward said, "Sam. Here's your life jacket." Sam reached the bow and turned to face Ward. He crossed his arms on his chest, his face defiant.

"Sam," said Laura, but Ward shook his head.

"Sammy," he said, "the rule is all people under four feet tall wear a life jacket."

"I'm not wearing one," Sam said. His eyebrows were knotted, his mouth tight. He clasped his shoulders with his hands, his elbows aimed out at the world.

"Well, you have to," Ward said.

"I'm not wearing that life jacket!" Sammy was screaming, his voice shrill and out of control. He had unfolded his arms, and as he screamed he beat his fists on his legs. *"I'm not wearing it, and you can't tell me to!"*

"Well, I'm the skipper, and I can," Ward said reasonably.

"Well, you *aren't* the skipper, and you *can't*." Sam's face was now scarlet, the blood flooding through the translucent skin.

"Sam, do *not* scream like that," Laura said. "You may *not* be so rude." Sam was backed up against the very smallest point of the bow. He had climbed onto the narrow seat in the prow. Everyone else was in the boat, and Ward had pulled up the anchor. Without it, the boat had begun to drift with the tide; it was pulled out into the channel between the two islands. Here the current was running strong, and they moved more and more rapidly as they met the full force of the tidal rush.

"Sam, I have to turn on the engine now, so we don't drift into something. But you must put on your life jacket. It's a rule, and you must obey it." Ward was brusque. He glanced from Sam to the channel, watching for shoals, then back to the furious child.

"Turn *on* the engine! Turn *on* the engine!" Sam screamed, throwing his hand toward Ward as though he were throwing rocks at him. The boat rocked, as a patch of wind shifted the water they were in, and Sammy tipped on his narrow pedestal. Laura began moving toward him.

"Sam, get down here this minute," she said. "That's enough of this screaming."

"Get away from me!" Sammy said, hysterical. He was overtired, he was on that tightrope of frenzied exhaustion where children teeter, far outside their own control, wild with tension and unhappiness, vibrating like electric wires. Laura stepped over the seat where Pia and Karin balanced, round-faced and solemn.

"Don't you come near me!" Sam screamed, waving ferociously at her. The boat veered away from the other island and began picking up speed toward the Western Way.

"*Don't* you talk to your mother like that," Ward said, now entirely engaged. "You stay where you are, Laura," Ward said. "Sam and I have to talk this out." He put the engine in neutral, left the stern and began clambering over the seats toward Sammy. Sammy stood up again, his feet set as wide as he could get them.

"Don't you touch me," screamed Sammy, punching with both hands toward Ward. *"Only my mother and my father can touch me! And my mother is still married to my father!"*

He was so brave, Laura thought, his small body wild and tiny against the wide horizon beyond, like the screaming gulls in the empty sky.

As Ward got closer Sam got more frantic.

"*No*! NO!" he screamed, punching the air in Ward's direction. But Ward, his face set, was now angry. He had never met Sammy head-on before; Laura had always come between them. But she could see it was inevitable, and that she could do nothing. Oh, Ward and his rules again, she thought, her eyes on her sons's small brave figure against the choppy water. But her easy, anarchic response no longer worked. This time she agreed with Ward and his rules. Ward stepped carefully in between Sarah and Richie. The boat wavered violently, and Ward crouched to steady it. Sammy teetered, and reached cautiously down for the gunwales. As Ward stood again so did Sammy. Ward said nothing, but stepped steadily toward the furious child, the big, orange life jacket in his hands. He reached Sammy, who stood now on tiptoes in his rage, his face contorted and violent.

"Put it on, Sam, and shut up. Don't you scream at me or your mother." Ward held out the life jacket. His own legs were spread against the uncertain set of the boat, and, standing in front of the child, he was massive, inescapable. He blocked Sammy from Laura, and she leaned anxiously outside the boat to see her son. The boat rocked; Sammy made a tiny leap, punching out at Ward; Ward thrust the life jacket at him; Sammy's sneaker slipped on the wet seat and his body made a slow cartwheel through the air. The splash was surprisingly small, as though a small rock had fallen into the water. Laura could not move for a long time; she felt herself willing her legs, her arms to start, but for a long time she was motionless, with that wild slow cartwheel against the blue water, that deadly, small splash. Ward had lunged as Sammy went into the air; he was still sprawled against the prow, trying to push himself away. Laura could hear nothing from Sammy, she could not see him in the water—he was on the other side of the boat from her—she still could not move.

While she was still willing herself to move she found she was taking off her sweater, for a moment she was blinded and struggling against her own gestures, her sneakers were off too and she felt the side of the boat hit her thigh hard, she had ricocheted against Richie, climbing diagonally across the boat in a straight line for where Sammy had last been, she still had not heard any sound from him and she threw herself into the water clumsily, knocking her hip, scraping her hands, her ribs: the boat, parts of the boat were in her way and she could not even look at them as she threw them aside, threw them all from her until she was free and deep in the frozen, frozen surge. She struggled through the water; it was so *heavy,* she had never known that it was so heavy to move through but she got her legs, her arms, to get her through to where Sammy should have been. But the boat must have drifted in that endless time she had taken to get moving, to get across the boat and out of it, and she looked around the shifting gray green waves that slid up in front of her, blocking her view. Then where was he? She had only that thought. She struggled toward the boat again, thinking he was on the other side of it. Ward was standing in the prow and shouting something but she could not understand him; she was angry at him for making no sense. She kicked and thrashed in the water, throwing herself in a circle, looking around again at the water that surrounded her, that blocked her sight, that held her son. She slapped at the waves, and heard her name. Ward was shouting at her, and she looked wildly up at him. What did he want? He was now in the stern of the boat, by the engine. He pointed, he pointed as though he threw a spear, into the water a few yards away from her. She could see nothing but the rocking waves, the breeze had come up more, and the waves were white and choppy. She beat at them, kicking her way through. The water came up salt in her throat; she opened her eyes too soon and was blinded. It did not feel cold, she had no feeling at all. Her hands felt useless, they were so small against the big water around her. She swam on and on; she kicked, spitting water, and felt something ahead of her. She grabbed it; it slipped away, she went for it as though it were the last breath of her life.

She pulled Sammy's head up out of the water. His eyes were closed and he was heavy, much heavier than he should be, all those arms and legs, she thought—jeans, sweater, sneakers—she must have everything in her hands. She pulled his head as far as she could get it out of the water. She was holding on to Sammy's shoulder; it slipped away; she grabbed again beneath his armpit. His head flopped loose in the water. Sammy's face was bluish white, the water covering it as though it belonged there. His eyes were shut, his mouth rolled loosely open.

The boat was behind her, the motor running cautiously. She churned herself around and found hands extended to her. She chose Ward's; she took his hand in one of hers and found herself lifted through the air, with Sammy clutched under her shoulder, as though she were a fish on a line, as though she were no weight at all. The boat beneath her feet was hard but unsteady. She sat down with Sammy half across her lap. She stretched him out flat on his back on the seat and stood, straddling the seat and Sammy's legs, holding them firmly between her own. She set her hands against his small, brave, arching ribs. Ward's face was next to Sammy's, his mouth near the boy's. Laura pushed down into the ribs for a long, slow moment. The timing she knew instinctively: the lifesaving course she had taken, long ago, had risen miraculously and taken over. She knew exactly what to do; each thought, each gesture would be the right one. When she could press no further, she paused. Water, clear and untroubled, moved suddenly out of Sammy's mouth, spilling easily over his cheek. What if there were more water inside? Could Ward put air in his lungs if there were still more water inside?

Ward pushed her gently away. He took Sammy by the ankles, his hands fitting neatly around the sodden, blue black jeans, and held him upside down. Sam's arms swung horribly loose. His fingers brushed against the floor of the boat. "Pat him on the back," Ward said urgently. Laura understood the sentence quite easily. She put her hand against Sam's back and thumped gently.

Ward was watching Sam's mouth. "More," he said, "again." Water was streaming out in a loose, liquid surge. Laura hit Sam again on the back, feeling the sodden wrinkles of his jersey beneath her hand, the solid flat stretch of rib and muscle, the small meek depression on either side of the spine.

"Now," Ward said, and laid Sam's shape along the seat in front of Laura again.

Laura straddled Sammy's body, and leaned forward again. Again she fitted her hands onto the neat arc of the ribs. Stretched out on the seat before her, Sammy glistened, his skin and clothes were coated with a thin layer of fluid, reflective light, like a pebble in a tidal pool. The glitter was wrong, unearthly, and it frightened Laura. Leaning forward, putting her weight slowly onto the fragile cavity of his chest, she could not bear for the water to have coated him so easily, to remain there gleaming, as though it were final.

She pushed slowly against his chest, feeling, with her hands, the rhythm of her own breathing, willing an answering rhythm within his torso. While she pressed she watched Sam's face. It was pale, as though it had never seen light, ever. The skin was translucent, the shadows on it blue, and the nostrils had fallen in toward each other, as though a passage for air were no longer necessary. The dense fan of eyelashes made a spiky huddle on the sweet semicircle below the eye. And the mouth: Sammy's mouth looked to Laura as though it had just that moment been finished, the edges sharp and perfectly defined, its ample shape spilling precisely along the curve. It was the water, still welling capriciously out, that was wrong. Each time Laura paused, Ward fitted his mouth over Sammy's, his head obscuring the boy's, enclosing the small face, and the warm soft air from Ward's lungs entered Sammy's.

When there was no air left in Ward's chest, he raised his

head again. Laura was crouched over Sammy, listening, her whole body focused, waiting for a deep, silent beat from the center of him. Listening, she waited—Ward next to her—her breath held, her eyes fixed on Sammy's, so that when, the lids beating uncertainly before the sudden, smooth widening, her son opened his eyes, he saw the faces that had brought him there.

Linn Sage

We started taking our family to Mount Desert Island, Maine, in the summer of 1979. Since then we've gone back nearly every summer, sometimes renting a house, sometimes chartering a sailboat and cruising along the coast, island to island. I love that part of Maine: the raking northern light against those old white clapboard houses. The clarity of the air, and the feel of it, fresh and tingling. The smooth bare rounded slopes that rise from Mount Desert. I love the silence of the small islands, and the dark blue water, cold and deep.